Dream

your

ECHOES
From The
PAST

ECHOES
from The
PAST

Dirk Pool

authorHOUSE®

AuthorHouse™
1663 Liberty Drive
Bloomington, IN 47403
www.authorhouse.com
Phone: 1 (800) 839-8640

© 2015 Dirk Pool. All rights reserved.

No part of this book may be reproduced, stored in a retrieval system, or transmitted by any means without the written permission of the author.

Published by AuthorHouse   07/17/2015

ISBN: 978-1-5049-1531-1 (sc)
ISBN: 978-1-5049-1530-4 (e)

Print information available on the last page.

Image used under license from Shutterstock.com

This book is printed on acid-free paper.

Because of the dynamic nature of the Internet, any web addresses or links contained in this book may have changed since publication and may no longer be valid. The views expressed in this work are solely those of the author and do not necessarily reflect the views of the publisher, and the publisher hereby disclaims any responsibility for them.

Dedicated To Bobbie

CHAPTER ONE

THE BEAMS OF SUNLIGHT, that filtered through the cracks between the slats in the vinyl blinds at the Valley View Motel, danced along the grey carpeted floor, as the ceiling fan gently swayed the blinds to and fro. The sun, bathing the western sky in lavishing colours of pink, yellow, and blue, tinted the few fluffy white clouds in an array of splendour. While all nature below stood in awe of all this beauty, Katelyn Melroy, the evening desk clerk, was too busy with her nose buried in a history book to even notice such radiance displayed in the western sky.

Katelyn, was twenty-two years old with reddish brown hair and smokey grey eyes. Her light brown complexion revealed her love for the outdoors. Although she worked as a motel desk clerk, she had put herself through university and achieved a BA in History. At age thirteen, Katelyn had started working at the Motel on weekends as a housekeeper. From there she had worked her way up to being an evening desk clerk. She had earned enough money to put herself through University, after finishing high school. Now that she had her degree, her hearts desire was to pursue her life as a Historian. She volunteered her time in the local Galt Museum to get closer to her dream.

Only a few days before, Rolland her boyfriend had taken her to see the movie, "Titanic," and she had cried through most of the three hours and fifteen minutes that it had played. Rolland had laughed about it, but he understood the real feelings that Katelyn had about the Titanic. She didn't cry because of the love story portrayed in the movie, but rather because of all the lives that had been snuffed out unnecessarily. After that, Katelyn had gone to the library to do some research about what had really happened to the Titanic. She had checked out the book she was studying because it was filled with interesting things that had taken place in this historic event. Although the movie portrayed a love story, much of the story was also taken right out of the history books.

Katelyn was so captivated by the history behind Titanic, that she never noticed the door opening and the man approaching the counter. When he spoke he startled her back to reality. It was like coming from yesteryear back to present time.

"Excuse me Miss.," he spoke quietly, but yet politely.

Katelyn, looking dazed for a moment, and realizing where she was, blushed sheepishly as she tried to contain her embarrassment. How could she have let herself get so deeply involved with the history of the Titanic that she became oblivious to her surroundings? She would have to be more attentive to her work whenever her nose was buried in a history book while on the job.

"I'm sorry Sir," she spoke nervously as she glanced up at the man standing at the counter, facing her. "I didn't see you come in."

"That was obvious Miss." the man grinned back at her. "That must be quite the book you are reading, for you to get so lost in it."

Realizing that this gentleman was not one bit upset, but rather enjoyed the moment of surprise, Katelyn relaxed as she explained what she had been reading. The man seemed pleased to hear her explanation, and didn't even hurry her along as she pleasantly relayed the history she was presently studying.

Katelyn was one of those people who would get lost in her thoughts as she dreamed about the history she was studying. Although she was not negligent about her work, if Katelyn was busy with something that interested her, she would just put other things off until her mind came back to what she was doing. Getting involved with her reading at work didn't happen too often, even though she read often during the down times on slow nights. This was just one of those times that the history she was reading had taken her back to that event. Even at the museum Katelyn could let herself drift off into the time period she was working on. She so longed for the day that being a desk clerk would be over and she could be a full time Historian. Her dream was to work in the Victoria Museum.

No matter what history she was studying, Katelyn let her imagination engulf her into that time frame. Even as she explained what had transpired in her brain to the man standing before her, her face beamed with anticipation of what must have taken place those last moments before the Titanic sank beneath the surface of that freezing cold water.

As she shared her deepest thoughts with the gentleman, the door opened and a young woman came in carrying a bag which she clutched tightly to her chest. She looked a bit lost, or maybe even somewhat scared. Her unkempt hair, which hung loosely about her shoulders, matched her unwashed face. The soiled clothes, drapping carelessly over her body, were badly in need of replacement. Walking over to the lobby, she plopped herself into one of the comfortable high-back chairs, and then began toying nervously with her hands after placing the bag on her lap. Getting up from the chair, and clutching the bag tightly to her bosom, she went to the vending machine. Staring aimlessly at it for a moment, she returned to the chair, and once more plopped herself carelessly into it, all the while her eyes were darting back and forth as though she was afraid to be seen there.

Katelyn resumed her talk with the man at the counter, while keeping her eye on the young woman. When she had gotten up to go to the vending machine, Katelyn couldn't help feeling a bit sympathetic towards this vagabond. She noticed how the young woman clutched the bag as though all her life's possessions were contained in that one bag. There seemed to be a feeling in her gut that there might be more to this young woman than met the eye. Although she felt sorry for her, Katelyn was also annoyed at the thought that this young woman might think that she could spend the night sleeping in one of the lobby chairs.

Excusing herself for a moment from the man at the counter, she directed her attention to the girl. "Is there something I can help you with Miss." Katelyn addressed her sternly.

"I need a room," came the nervous reply.

"I'll be with you shortly," Katelyn spoke feeling a bit uneasy about her. What would someone like her be doing in a high classed motel like this one.

Turning back to the customer at the counter, she apologized to him for boring him with her history tales. She explained that she was just so excited about history, that it was part of her life.

"That's okay Miss.," he spoke reassuringly. "I enjoyed listening to you."

"I know that you didn't come in here to listen to me talk. Are you by yourself?"

"Yes. I have a reservation for a room for the night. My name is Joe Flaxton."

When Katelyn heard the name, she nearly fell over backwards. She had been informed that Mr. Flaxton would be staying at the motel for the night, and that he was a very distinguished businessman. He was travelling to Edmonton, from Great Falls Montana and was stopping at Lethbridge, Calgary, and Red Deer, on his way to Edmonton to check on clothing stores that he owned in each one of these cities.

"Mr. Flaxton," Katelyn spoke apologetically, "I am so sorry that I kept you waiting while I rambled on about my interests."

"Don't be sorry Miss.," Flaxton smiled at her. "It isn't everyday that I get the opportunity to listen to someone tell me about their interests."

"But I shouldn't be boring an important man like yourself with my life." Katelyn continued.

"My life is so full of running around because of my stores that I seldom get time to listen to others tell of their life. This was very relaxing after the trip from Great Falls."

Flaxton got the key from Katelyn and reassured her that it had been a great pleasure to hear her talk about the Titanic. She thanked him for his pleasant consideration and understanding, and as he turned to leave, she centred her attention on the young woman in the lobby chair. She looked so out of place in the motel. Her long dirty blond hair, hanging recklessly down her back and over her shoulders, appeared as though she hadn't done anything with it in days. Katelyn motioned her to the counter. Her unwashed face, appeared to be streaked from much crying. She was hesitant, but when she finally got up the courage to approach Katelyn, her eyes were darting back and forth like a caged animal. She once more clutched her bag as though it were her one and only prized possession.

"I need a room for the night," she spoke fearfully as she looked at the floor.

"That will be fifty dollars," Katelyn said wondering if the young woman had the means to pay for the room.

Pulling a roll of money from her pocket, she proceeded to peel off fifty dollars. Then taking the pen Katelyn offered her, she filled in the required card. The name she wrote was, Jill Smith, and the address was just Calgary, Alberta.

"Don't you have a street address and phone number?" Katelyn asked.

Looking at Katelyn through fear filled eyes, Jill swallowed hard before replying. It looked as though she was ready to break down and cry.

"Please don't make me write down my real name and address," Jill suddenly burst into tears.

Katelyn felt at loss about what to do. She wasn't a counsellor, and nothing like this had ever happened to her before. In all the years that she had been a clerk, she had known of men and women staying at the motel under different names, but never had anyone broken into tears before. Katelyn felt that it was none of her business if men and women cheated on their spouses, as long as it never happened to her after she got married. She had decided a long time ago that her husband would never be given any reason to want someone else.

"It's okay," Katelyn tried to sound reassuring. "Jill Smith is all the name that we need."

"Thank you," Jill sobbed. "If a man comes in here looking for me and gives my description, please don't let him know I'm here."

"Nobody but myself will ever know that you are here," Katelyn promised her.

CHAPTER TWO

AFTER JILL LEFT, KATELYN couldn't help but wonder what a young woman like her could be running away from. Maybe she had a father who beat her and abused her. It wouldn't be a husband, because she couldn't be much older than seventeen. The thought of such a young woman running for fear of her life bothered Katelyn. What possessed people to want to hurt some other human being? It just didn't make any sense, but then again, so many things in life today didn't make any sense. Katelyn was thankful that she had been interested in history, because that way she could learn about the ways and means of those who had lived in bygone days. Life way back then, seemed to be a lot less complicated than it was today. Sure, they had their problems too, but they seemed to cope with problems better than how the society of today coped.

As Katelyn pondered over the problems of the world of today, she began to wish that she had been born a few generations earlier. If only we could go back to the time before steam engines had been invented, or the telephone and electricity. These things were all nice, but it seemed as though life started to pass by much quicker after these things had been introduced into the world. Just imagine all those romantic candle light dinners people must have had. Katelyn thought about Rolland, her boyfriend, taking her by the arm and leading her to a table filled with candle light. As they approached the chair she was to be sitting in, he would pull it out for her and help her get into place before heading for his own chair. He would smile at her from across the dinner table while possibly making romantic gestures to her. Just the thought of such a life happening to her caused Katelyns heart to skip a beat. Yes, it would be so nice to live back in those days, but with the coming of television, and computers, life had taken on a totaly different meaning.

Back then, after a wonderful dinner, Rolland would possibly take her out onto the floor and dance the evening away. The music would be soft, but yet thrilling, romantic and breath taking. As Rolland spun her around, Katelyn's dress would billow out and then twirl as if in time with the music. They would glide across the floor as though they were floating on clouds. People would look at them in awe and admiration, as dance after dance, Rolland swept her along breathlessly into the night.

Just the thought of dancing with Rolland in such an old fashioned setting was enough to take Katelyn's breath away, at that moment. With her imagination running wild the way it did, Katelyn never seemed to get bored with life. Hers was a life of adventure without really being there. It didn't cost anything to travel into yesteryear, especially with a mind set like Katelyn had. In fact, she felt sorry for people who couldn't live in dreams.

At least two hours had gone by without even a phone call for reservations, but Katelyn didn't mind. This was Friday, and it was unusually quite slow for the end of the week, but it had been a good night to have no disturbances in her dream world. At times it could get boring, but this definitely had not been at all boring for Katelyn. On the contrary, her mind had drifted off into the past, so for her benefit it was a good thing that the night had been as slow as it was.

Her thoughts and dreams were shattered as a beautiful young girl entered the lobby. She headed for the vending machine and after dropping in her money, she took out a can of pop and then repeated the procedure. With the two cans of pop in her hands, she approached the counter. The girl looked vaguely familiar, but Katelyn couldn't place her. As she came near, Katelyn realized that it was Jill. She had taken a bubble bath, and the sweet fragrance filled the air. Her hair, now glimmering in the light, no longer hung loosely about her neck, but it was done up in ringlets. The vagabonds clothing had been replaced by a new dress. The eyes that looked at Katelyn, although still showing signs of anxiety as they darted about, were beautiful hazel eyes that highlighted her beauty. Katelyn believed that those very eyes would sparkle if fear were removed from them.

"I'm sorry for carrying on the way I did," she said as she placed the pop on the counter. "I believe that I owe you an explanation."

"You don't have to tell me anything if you don't want to," Katelyn spoke reassuringly to her. "We all live our lives differently."

"I know," Jill began, "But I just feel in my heart that I should share this with you."

"If it will make you feel better," Katelyn said, not wanting to pry into Jill's affair. If she needed to talk to get something off her chest, then Katelyn would sit there and be her sounding board, even though she would rather read more about the Titanic.

"You sure became pretty since you first came into the motel," Katelyn tried to sound reassuring.

"Thank you," Jill cracked a smile. "I have felt so dirty the last couple months, that I decided this would be a good time to change."

Katelyn had been right, Jill was just barely seventeen. At the age of sixteen she had run away from home and had lived off the streets till just a few months ago. She had met this thirty-six year old man who convinced her that she was the best thing that ever happen to him since sliced bread. He had been a smooth talker, and before Jill knew it, they were living together. Since Jill had been living on the streets before getting involved with this man, the idea of living in a house and having her own man all seemed so nice. Everything had gone alright the first month, and then he began coming home drunk. He would beat her and demand from her more and more work around the house. If she even slipped up a little bit, he would beat her even more. She found out through one of his drunken stupors that he was married, but that his wife had left him. Jill had finally become fed up with the way she was being treated, and taking the money that he had in his pants pocket, she had fled the house that evening. He had passed out on the kitchen floor, and seizing the opportunity, Jill had checked his pockets and had found the wad of money that she had paid the room with. Before coming to the motel, she had gone out and bought the dress she was wearing, plus all the toiletries and make up to go with it. On top of it, she had purchased a nice curling iron. She told Katelyn that it was her intention to go back home to her parents in Calgary and letting them know that she was wrong in running away from home. Life at home had been much better than the life she had experienced the past few months. Running away from home had seemed like such a good thing to do at the time, but now she was ready to run back home.

At least at home she had clean cloths to wear, good food to eat, and a warm comfortable bed to sleep in. Life on the streets was not what she had thought it would be. She had experienced freedom from rules and regulations, but that freedom had come at a great cost. Many times she had gone hungry and at nights she would find cardboard to sleep under. The street bums she associated with, were of no help since they were trying to look out for themselves. Even though life on the streets had been hard, Jill had been unable to find it in her heart to call her parents to admit that she was wrong and that she was sorry for running away. It had been the life with a drunk that had woke her up to realize that her life could be much better if her parents would forgive her.

After telling Katelyn what was on her heart, Jill seemed so much more at ease, except that her eyes still held fear that the drunk she had been with would find her. Katelyn promised her that she would be safe at the motel, and that nobody would find her there. Jill smiled and thanked Katelyn for her help, and her listening ear. It takes all kinds, Katelyn thought as Jill headed back to her room.

The rest of her shift was quiet, and Katelyn was able to read more about the history of the Titanic. She was into the part where over fifteen hundred people lost their lives, and her eyes filled with tears. How could man be so stupid? All those people lost their lives because it was man that thought the ship would look nicer with less life boats. It had been a very reckless decision on the part of those men to decide that they would never need the life boats anyway. It had always been man's desire and quest for more power and more speed.

The pyramids of Egypt had been built by slaves, many slaves whose lives meant nothing to the pharaoh. So what if they lost a few hundred slaves in the process of building bigger and better empires. Slaves had been used to row the mighty sailing ships that travelled abroad in the waters of the Roman Empire days. It was a hard job for those slaves as overseers cut their backs with whips if they stopped rowing. As the slaves died rowing these mighty ships, others would replace them at the oars, only to be replaced themselves as they lost their life at the hands of another human. Many slaves lost their lives while in chains they rowed battle ships into watery graves.

As man progressed in time, and things began to grow faster with more power required to operate the machines that were invented, the regard for another humans life did not change. Bigger and better equipment was being used in mines, causing bigger cave ins and more lives buried beneath tons of dirt and rocks. Corners would be cut in order to save time and money with no thought of the lives that were at stake with these cutbacks. The big shots were getting richer while many wives and children would never see their husbands and fathers again.

World War I and World War II took the lives of thousands of soldiers and civilians alike, just because someone thought they could rule the world. In order to overthrow these forces in power, men and women fought these rulers to gain freedom for other who would come after them. These men and women died so that the world could remain living free lives. Although Hitler fought hard to gain control of the world, Germany also lost many lives fighting for this insane man.

Throughout the history of mankind, there had always been battles between nations and countries to gain control. If only man could live in peace together, then the world would be a better place to live.

When the space age came into being, and time was flying by, men still lost their lives. Three astronauts died as their rocket burned without even lifting off the ground. Bigger and better rockets were built and sent out into space faster and faster all the time. Less and less concentration was being put on the value of human lives as these rockets were being produced. With their hearts and minds intent on sending yet another crew of astronauts into orbit, seven people lost their lives on January 28, 1986, because of human error not wanting to waste another moment of precious time. Instead of wasting so called precious time, seven people, who were loved by their families, would not be seen by their loved ones again. That also had been a tragic time in the history of mankind.

Air planes come crashing to the ground because of some malfunction due to improper maintenance, perhaps because of cut backs. On June 17, 1996 at approximately 2:15 P.M. Value Jet Flight 592 crashed into the Florida Everglades causing 110 lives to be snuffed out. This was only one more situation where human error caused the death of other humans. There were numerous situations where people died in plane crashes because of negligent decisions.

There had been many train disasters where people were hurt or killed. One that came to Katelyn's mind was the one near London England where seven passengers had lost their lives, plus at least 147 others were injured. That happened September 20, 1997 when the 1032 Great Western Intercity High Speed Train crashed into an empty freight train. These were all unnecessary deaths that could have been prevented had someone not been in such a hurry to let the freight train cross the tracks of the oncoming Great Western. Would mankind ever stop to consider the value of another human being.

Katelyn wiped the tears from her eyes and also from the side of her face. She was certainly getting involved tonight with the history of the human race. It was not that she was angry or upset with the lives that it had cost to get where we were today, it was just the thought of who would have to sacrifice their life next so that humanity could go on. Was there no way that things could progress without life being snuffed out in order to achieve the goal of success?

Rolland entered into the lobby and Katelyn realized that it was almost time for the night clerk to take over. Soon she would be here, and Katelyn could leave with Rolland and go to some nice quiet place for coffee. Every Friday evening he would pick her up from work because he could sleep in the next day since he didn't work on the weekends. This had been an exhilarating night of travelling around in history for Katelyn, with her imaginary adventurous mind, and she just wanted her shift to end. She would be so thrilled if she was eccepted into the Victoria Museum. The bliss of that thought sent shivers up and down her spine. In her mind, she could be lost forever amongst the artifacts in that Museum.

As he came up to the counter, Rolland could see that Katelyn had been in tears. He cracked a smile as he looked at her and gently took her face into his hands. While placing a kiss on the end of her nose, he remarked, "Reliving history again, Sweetie!"

Rolland was twenty five years old, with dark hair, that went well with his brown eyes. Spending four nights a week at the gym, Rolland kept fit and was in good shape. There was no visible fat anywhere on his body. He worked for a major accounting firm in the city, and he was so good at his job that many times he would be called upon to go to other towns or cities to work on clients books. He cared a great deal about Katelyn, and dreamed someday to marry her.

Although Rolland had different interests than Katelyn did, he respected her desire to study history. They had been together for nearly one year, and it gave him great pleasure to be near Katelyn. He enjoyed seeing her deep in thought about some historical event. He knew that she would dream about that time period, and in her mind, actually live it out.

Katelyn blushed with embarrassment because she had not been able to hide her feelings of the night from Rolland. He was such a loving and caring man, and even though he didn't share in the interests of history, he supported Katelyn in her desires to know more about the way things were in the past. He would maybe joke about the history of mankind, but he would never think of hurting Katelyns feelings about how she thought. Katelyn felt well protected whenever Rolland was around. If she cried about the way things were, or had been, Rolland would always reassure her that he was behind her all the way. It was funny how things were between the two of them. They were so different in their likes and dislikes, but yet they were very compatible. Just like two magnets, opposite poles attract while like poles repelled. Many couples looked for a mate with all the same likes and dislikes. In many of those cases the relationship fell apart so often, Katelyn thought as relief flooded her face. She could finally leave and spend a few minutes with her beloved over a cup of coffee. The Titanic and other dissaters could be laid to rest for a while.

The night clerk, Tracy, had entered the lobby and she noticed Katelyn's tear streaked face. Hearing what Rolland had just said she understood what had taken place. Tracy had become very close to Katelyn, and she knew how Katelyn desired to get a job where her degree in history would pay off. Tracy admired Katelyn for the dedication she had for the study of history. Although she hated to see Katelyn go, at the same time she hoped that there would be an opening for Katelyn in the area that she had studied so hard to receive a degree in.

"Had a rough night tonight Katelyn?" Tracy teased.

"I just got myself too involved with the history of the Titanic tonight," Katelyn replied. "As well as thinking about many other disasters caused by man's neglect."

"Well," Tracy chuckled as she looked at Katelyns face, "Why don't you go freshen up and the two of you go for coffee together."

"It's not quite eleven o'clock yet," Katelyn objected.

"Never mind that now," Tracy playfully scolded her as she winked at Rolland, "You can't let the Knight who has come to rescue you, stand waiting. Go now and I will cover for you."

"Thank you Tracy. I owe you one," Katelyn patted Tracy's arm lightly.

"What are friends for," Tracy playfully taunted. "Besides, you have covered for me often enough when due to dificulties I couldn't make it to work on time."

After she got refreshed, Katelyn grabbed her coat and purse. She couldn't help but feel a warm glow in her heart. Rolland made her feel like she was somebody special. No other guy had ever had that kind of affect on her. They had known each other for less than a year, but it was enough time to realize that they made a perfect couple. That is, if there was such a thing. They were outside next to Rolland's car and Katelyn watched as he unlocked and opened her door for her. Rolland was that kind of man. He always tried to do things for Katelyn. It didn't matter whether they were big things or little things. Some of the things that Rolland did for her would seem insignificant to most men, but to Rolland, they meant the world. As long as it made Katelyn happy.

"I sure do love you Rolland," Katelyn whispered to him.

"Sweetie," Rolland looked directly into her smoky grey eyes, "You are the only one for me. My heart throbs when I am near you"

"Oh Rolland," Katelyn blushed, "You are such a wonderful man. Daily I long to feel your strong arms around me in loving embrace, while the gentleness of your kisses cause my knees to go weak. My Love, you are so caring and understanding. My heart throbs as well when you hold me tight."

They embraced each other for a few moments before their lips met. Fires of passion tore through Katelyn, like a thousand lightning bolts, as she momentarily lost control of her senses. Rolland gently pulled away from her so as not to be put into an embarrassing situation. He desired to have Katelyn, but he would remembered the promise he had made to her as long as he lived. They would refrain from going too far unless they were married.

"I think we better go get some coffee," Rolland smiled at the bewildered Katelyn.

"Rolland my Love," Katelyn sighed with relief, "You sure know how to arouse a young girls hormonal passions."

"You are a young lady, not a young girl," Rolland teased her, "You are the only young lady I want in my life. As for arousal, you make it hard for me to quit."

"Thank you for not letting me make a fool of myself," Katelyn placed a kiss on Rollands cheek before stepping into the car.

Very few words were spoken as they drove to the restaurant. They both had thoughts of the love they had for the other. Katelyn desired for Rolland to ask her to marry him, while Rolland, even though he desired to marry Katelyn, wanted her to pursue her dream first. He was not to sure how he would even approach her about marriage. He thought she might refuse the proposal because of her dream, although in his heart he believed differently. He figured she might let her dream go just for the sake of marrying him, or maybe he was just to chicken to ask her.

While they spent a few moments together in the restaurant, Katelyn couldn't help but think back at the candle light dinner she had dreamed about earlier. She shared that with Rolland, and as usual he teased her about her dreams. She knew that he was just jesting her, and she smiled at him. Not once throughout the evening did she mention anything to Rolland about Jill. It wasn't that she didn't trust him, she had promised Jill that no one would know that she was staying at the motel. There would be plenty of time after she was gone to mention it to Rolland. He would understand like always why she had not rushed into telling him about the incident.

After they had finished their coffee, they left the restaurant and like always, Rolland opened the car door for her. Katelyn thought better of kissing him this time. She felt a warm fire burning in her bosom, and she couldn't trust herself tonight. Would it even be safe to kiss him goodnight, she wondered. When Rolland dropped her off at her place, Katelyn wasn't sure if she wanted to let him go. She felt so drawn to this man that she couldn't help thinking. Why hasn't he proposed to me yet? It was Rolland who leaned over and kissed her and she thought that her heart was going to explode. He must have sensed the danger they were in, because he didn't pressure Katelyn into a long romantic kiss. When he turned to leave, he remembered something he wanted to give to her.

"Sweetie," he looked lovingly and longingly into her eyes, "I have something for you, but you must close your eyes."

CHAPTER THREE

KATELYN'S HEART SKIPPED A beat as she closed her eyes and dreamt that Rolland was going to place an engagement ring on her finger. It felt like an eternity before he finally made his move. All the while her mind raced and her heart felt as though it would be torn apart with each second that passed by.

Along with her heart palpitating, Katelyn thought she was going to soar off into heavenly bliss as she stood waiting for that moment of ecstasy when her gallant knight in shining armour would sweep her off her feet by placing upon her finger the symbol of her being his forever. She had waited for this moment to come, not knowing how she would feel when it did happen.

Rollands voice seemed to be coming at her from some far away romantic island in the sea. "Now remember Sweetie, you must keep your eyes closed," he was saying.

Katelyn felt Rolland's body close to hers. She could smell the masculine aroma of his cologne, which caused tingles of anticipation to go through her whole body, as he embraced her for a moment before stepping back. She couldn't help wondering what Rolland was up to. She wanted to give him her hand so he could place the ring on her finger, but that would leave her feeling foolish if it wasn't a ring that he had for her. With her eyes closed tightly, it seemed like an eternity that she stood waiting. Katelyn knew from the smell of his cologne, that Rolland had moved behind her. She could feel Rollands body touching hers as he embraced her. Her breasts heaved with excitement as she felt his strong arms wrapped around her body, then he released his hold as he fidgeted with his hands for a moment. Katelyn could feel his arms moving slowly up her sides. Something was sliding up her chest, causing shivers of emotional passion to erupt from the very soles of her feet to the top of her head.

Suddenly, a cold object touched her skin below the neck line, causing her to gasp, but she managed to keep her eyes closed. Rolland was fastening a necklace around her neck, so it was not a ring he had for her. As he let go of the necklace, the cold object which slid down into her blouse, and settled between her breasts, sent chills up and down her spine.

"Okay," Rolland whispered in her ear before stepping back. "You can open your eyes now."

Reaching up with her hand, she took hold of the necklace and pulled out the cold object. In her hand she held a heart shaped locket which was attached to a golden necklace. The chain was long enough to allow her to open the locket and look inside. There were two small pictures in it. One was that of Rolland, and of course the other one was that of Katelyn. Rolland moved in front to face her.

Closing the locket, Katelyn threw her arms around Rolland's neck and then she began to cry. Burying her head on his shoulder, she just let the tears flow until the shoulder of his shirt was soaked. Rolland was just so good to her. Although it wasn't a ring that he gave her, Katelyn didn't want to push him into something that he might not feel ready for. At least his picture was in the locket opposite hers, and it hung next to her heart.

"Rolland," Katelyn sniffled as she spoke, "You are such a kind good hearted man. When I talk too much about the wonderful things in history, you patiently listen to me ramble on. Now you give me this beautiful locket with a picture of both of us in it. I will always treasure it as long as I live."

Hugging her close to himself, Rolland could feel his own heart beating rapidly. He wanted to ask Katelyn to marry him, but he feared that she might not be ready for such a proposal just yet. In his mind, she needed to see her dream come true first. There was still plenty of time, even though Rolland yearned to be with Katelyn and to hold her in his arms forever. Rollands biggest fear was that Katelyn would be moving away after getting excepted in Victoria. There were no real jobs in Lethbridge for the type of work she was looking for.

He would be happy for her, but by her leaving Rolland would be lonely without her. When she got eccepted to go to Victoria, he could of course always find a job there in his own field. Rolland decided to wait and see what happened with Katelyn first.

Although Rolland wasn't into history like Katelyn was, he respected her deep desires to be the best historian ever. Rolland was more into doing things like Martial Arts, and reading science fiction. Katelyn didn't care for those things, but she also supported Rolland in his interests.

After Rolland made sure Katelyn was safe in her own apartment, he drove away pleased that Katelyn liked the locket. Such things meant a lot to ladies, and he wanted to make sure that Katelyn always got the best. If only he could be certain what the future had in store for both of them. Maybe he was just a chicken to ask Katelyn to marry him. The worst she could do was to refuse, and then again, that wouldn't mean she didn't want him, just that she wasn't prepared to settle down at this particular time.

At nine o'clock the following morning, Katelyn was awakened by the ringing of the telephone. She had decided to sleep longer on this day. Reaching over to the night table, while still on her back, she fumbled for the receiver and dropped it to the floor. Rolling over on her side, she quickly retrieved the phone, and then sleepily answered, "Hello! I'm sorry! I dropped the phone."

"Katelyn, this is Mabel from work," the voice came over the receiver. "There is a girl here by the name of Jill who wants to talk to you."

"Okay," Katelyn yawned, "Put her on. I know who she is."

Katelyn was surprised that Jill would be calling her instead of getting a hold of her parents. Had something gone wrong? Did they not want her home because of what she had done? Maybe Jill had done more to her parents than what she had let on.

"Katelyn," Jill's voice came through the phone, "This is Jill. The girl from the Motel. Did I get you out of bed?" She sounded very frightened.

Fully awake by now, Katelyn politely answered, "I am still in bed, but that is okay. What can I do for you Jill?"

"I'm sorry to disturb you, but I didn't know who else to turn to for help, so I decided to call you." Jill spoke fearfully. "Of course they wouldn't give me your number, but offered to call you for me."

"What is it you need help with?" Katelyn requested.

"Can you meet me here so that we can talk?" Jill almost whispered.

Katelyns heart went out to Jill after the talk the night before. She wanted to see Jill get back home safely where her parents could look after her. The thought of having to live out on the street didn't appeal to Katelyn, and after seeing Jill all cleaned up and attractive, she hated to see her going back to that kind of life style, so she would do her best to see Jill safely on her way home.

"Did your parents reject you?" Katelyn wanted to know.

"I couldn't get through to them," Jill burst into tears.

"I'm sure there is an explanation," Katelyn spoke encouragingly. "I'll come to the Motel and then we can talk."

"Oh, I wish I hadn't been so stupid to leave my parents," Jill blubbered over the phone. "Maybe they hate me for what I have done. I don't deserve their love."

"Give me about an hour," Katelyn assured Jill. "I need to shower and then catch the bus."

"That's okay," Jill whispered, "I'll be in my room. I appreciate this, and will be forever in debt to you for it."

Katelyn couldn't even begin to imagine what it was that Jill wanted from her at this time. After last night, Katelyn knew that Jill needed to get home to her dad and mom. She had seen the light about street living, and had come to her senses. There was a good reason why Jill couldn't reach her parents at this time. Katelyn would lend her shoulder to Jill till she got through on the phone. After her shower, Katelyn decided to call a cab instead of taking the bus. That way she could at least get there much quicker. She didn't know why her heart went out to Jill, but for some reason she couldn't just let Jill fall by the wayside. Yes, Jill had made a foolish decision to leave home in a fit of rage, but there was something about her that Katelyn couldn't put her finger on. Never before had she desired to help someone succeed in life. Jill seemed to have touched her heart strings and she couldn't let it go.

Arriving at the Motel, Katelyn went straight over to Jill's room. After knocking softly on the door, she waited for an answer. It seemed like a long time before Jill finally answered the knock, after asking, "Who is it?"

"It's okay Jill, this is Katelyn,"

Fear was written all over her face as the door opened. She was trembling and Katelyn reached over to touch her but hugged her instead. She felt helpless as Jill burst into tears.

"What is it Jill?" Katelyn spoke soothingly to her.

"I want m–my dad and m-m-mom," Jill sobbed.

"That's okay," Katelyn tried to console her. "Why don't you try to call them again to let them know you are coming home?"

"I d-did ca-call," Jill continued to sob as she stammered. "But th-th-there was n-n-no answer. I've been ca–ca–calling ever since I ta–talked with y–you last n–n–night."

"I'm sure that there is something that we can do," Katelyn spoke reassuringly as she wrapped her arms tighter around Jill's shivering body.

Katelyn could not imagine what it was like not to be able to reach your parents in time of need. Her parents had always supported her in her dream of being a historian. They realized from Katelyn's early years, that history was in her blood.

"Wh-what else is th–there," Jill was wrought up with anxiety. The thought of living on the street again caused a haunting expression to shadow her face in a twisting motion of despair.

Katelyn was not sure what to do at this point in time, but she was sure that the answer would come to her. She had to calm Jill down enough to regain her confidence in being able to go back home to her dad and mom. Jill had told Katelyn that her real last name was Borden, and that her dad was an engineer who designed bridges and other sophisticated things to do with travel. It was very heart breaking to see someone who wanted to start over in life, find themselves alone without anywhere to turn. Katelyn was happy that she had always enjoyed a good home life, and that from a very young age she had already known what her plans were for the future. Now she was trying to console a girl who seemed to have no future.

Jill had slobbered all over Katelyn's blouse as she blubbered uncontrollably, and her tears added to the soaking. Last night her hopes of returning home had brought her into high spirits, but today her hopes were all gone by the wayside. She couldn't blame her parents for not being home. After all, it was Jill that had stormed out of the house, just over a year before, yelling at her parents, "I never want to see you again." Now she was stricken with grief over what she had done. She was sincerely sorry for ever having spoken to her parents that way.

Katelyn gently sat Jill down on the edge of the bed. Sitting down beside her, she placed one arm around Jill, while with the other hand she reached for the phone. An idea had come to her as she was standing holding Jill in her arms. In order to dial out, she had to release Jill for a moment, but after dialing the desired number, she once again placed her arm over Jill's shoulder to lend some much needed comfort to her

"Hello," Rollands voice came through the receiver.

"Honey," Katelyn replied, almost hesitantly, because of what she was about to ask him. "Could you please come meet me at the motel?"

Rolland was surprised to hear that Katelyn was at work. "Why? What's up?"

"I'll explain it all to you when you get here," Katelyn tried to sound cheery.

"Sure Sweetie," Rolland replied. "I'd be glad to meet you there."

While she waited with Jill for Rolland to arrive, Katelyn talked to Jill about staying at her apartment until she located her parents. There was no need to spend money at the Motel, and it would be safer for her at the apartment. She also informed her that they would have to wait in the sitting room so that the housekeeper could clean the room. Jill was nervous about leaving the room, but Katelyn assured her that it would be alright. Jill did not know how to respond to Katelyn's hospitality, and she burst into tears of gratitude. Her deepest desire was to turn her life around, and in the meantime she had found a new friend who was willing to put up with her until she succeeded in reaching her parents. She had done herself up again that morning, and Katelyn didn't think that anyone who knew her would even recognize her the way she looked that morning. She was a very attractive girl, and it almost made Katelyn envious of her. It didn't make sense to Katelyn why such a beautiful girl like Jill could even consider living out in the street. Then again, Jill probably never expected to start out on the street. Hard luck had placed her in that predicament when she had run away from her parents through a fit of rage.

People made rash decisions without thinking through the consequences of their conduct. The pasture that looked greener was not always as green as it looked from the other side. It never paid to make decisions when you were angry, because those times you always thought irrationally.

While they sat in the courtyard, overlooking the swimming pool, they drank coffee, and ate the continental breakfast together while Jill told Katelyn more about her past. Jill explained in more detail that her parents were very nice people. Her dad, being an engineer, designed bridges and tunnels that went under rivers and others over big bodies of water, just to mention a couple important things he did. The money he made was more than enough to supply Jill and her mother with the nice things in life, but her mom was a lawyer, and a very good one. So between her dad and mom bringing in the money, Jill had had it made. It was just that Jill had rebelled against them and picked the wrong kind of friends. These friends had turned out to be a hindrance in her life, because they were never there to help her in time of need. Jill was happy and thankful that Katelyn had not turned her back onto the street. In the year that she had been away from home, it was devastating to her life. She was ready to get under the rules and regulations of her dad and mom. Jill was just a normal teenager who went under, due to peer pressure. Her Parents sounded like very caring decent people. Jill agreed that it had been a very dumb move on her part, but at the same time it had been educational.

When Rolland arrived at the motel, Katelyn introduced Jill to him, and filled him in a little on her hard luck. She told Rolland that Jill would be spending the day at her place until she could get a hold of her parents. If need be, Jill would spend the night with Katelyn, and the next night as well until they reached Jill's parents. Jill was welcome to stay as long as she needed to.

They all got into Rolland's car, and back at the apartment, he reminded Katelyn about her appointment at one o'clock to go for her drivers licence. Through the excitement with Jill, Katelyn had forgotten about the appointment, but after settling Jill in, she was still on time to take the driver training test. On the way there, she explained in more detail to Rolland what had happened to Jill. Rolland was sympathetic and praised Katelyn for what she was doing.

As she took the driving test, Katelyn's head was buzzing with thoughts of Jill, but she managed to pay attention to the instructor, even though his voice seemed miles away. She passed without any problems, and Rolland rejoiced with her as she burst into tears of joy.

Since Katelyn had to work that evening, she gave Jill full reign of her apartment. She knew that Jill would be safe there and from what Jill had told her, Katelyn was assured that Jill wanted to stay inside, far from those who might recognize her. She promised Jill that she would call her later that evening to make sure that everything was still alright. If there was a problem, Jill was to call Katelyn immediately.

Even though it was Saturday, the evening at the motel was exceptionally quiet, as it had been the night before, so Katleyn decided to read a bit about the stage coach stopover she had heard about between Lethbridge and Fort Macleod. In fact, it had just been recently that she had heard someone mention there had been a stage coach between the two towns. Of course this was back when it was the town of Coalbanks later changed to Lethbridge. In 1881, William H Long came to Alberta, delivering a horse to a ranch in the Porcupine Hills.

He operated a ferry crossing near Fort Kipp, when he realized that he could build a ranch house as a stopover place for the stage coach that crossed the river near Fort Kipp on it's way to and from Fort Macleod and Coalbanks. The stage coach would leave Fort Macleod at 9:00 a.m., stop at the Ranch House for lunch at noon, and get into Coalbanks by evening.

The stopover served well, and when Long's friend, Richard Urch arrived in 1884 to help run the ranch, they decided to build a larger house. Long and Urch built a two story ranch house in 1886, and between the stage coach, bull train drivers, and occasionally some of the North West Mounted Police coming over, many hungry people were being fed at the ranch house. Katelyn wondered what it would have been like running a stopover house where meals were served to all those hungry people.

She could not find a lot of information on the subject of the stopover house, so it was hard for her to even dream anything up about it. Just the fact that Coalbanks and

Fort Macleod had a stage running between them was amazing in itself. Katelyn had always pictured stage coaches in the wild west stories of the States. Never had it occurred to her that such a thing could have happened right here in the province of Alberta.

It was not until the next morning that Jill finally got in touch with her parents. They were so excited to hear her voice, that her dad said they were coming straight over to Lethbridge to pick her up. Tears of joy streamed down Jill's face as she hung up the phone. She looked over at Katelyn, but couldn't even speak the gratitude she had for Katelyn letting her spend the night with her. She wanted to express how thankful she was that Katelyn had taken the time to talk to her, but words just seemed to evade her at that moment, as tears streamed down her face.

Katelyn, with tears of joy streaming down her own face, reassured Jill that it was okay to cry, and that she didn't have to try and talk. It was understandable that Jill would be to chocked up to speak. Just knowing that she was returning home to her loving parents was triumphant enough for Katelyn. They embraced each other and just let the tears flow for a few minutes, and then Katelyn called Rolland on his cell to give him the good news.

"Honey," Katelyn burst into a new array of tears, "I'm sorry to bother you, but Jill contacted her parents."

"That's wonderful Sweetie," Rolland didn't know what else to say because he was busy working on a clients contract which he had taken home with him to work on over the weekend.

"I know you are working on that contract, but I just had to call and let you know that Jill's parents are coming to Lethbridge to pick her up this afternoon at about 4:00," Katelyn continued with excitement. "They were so happy to hear her voice, that they never even said anything about her running away from home."

Although Rolland was working hard to finish the contract, he still liked the idea of having a small break from all the figures. He informed Katelyn, after some small talk, that he was going to take time off from the contract so that they could pick up the car that Katelyn had her heart set on. Now that she had her licence, there was no reason why she couldn't have a car of her own. Katelyn agreed, and after hanging up the phone, she told Jill what they were planning to do. Jill was excited for Katelyn, and wished her the best with her new car. Katelyn and Jill rejoiced together for a couple hours for each others happiness, until Rolland's knock came at the door.

They made the trip to the car lot, and Katelyn purchased the car that she had desired to have for at least a week. They had figured that she would pass the drivers test, so Rolland had gone with her to look at cars. Katelyn had spotted the car of her dreams, and to make sure that the salesman couldn't sell it, she had put a deposit down and got the paper work done on it.

Together they went to get insurance for the car, and to register it. The place where Rolland had his car insured was open on Saturdays and Sundays from noon till three in the afternoon, for those who couldn't make it during the week. After that, Katelyn insisted that they take her car for a nice drive down the road. Rolland agreed, and they spent a couple hours just touring around so that Katelyn could get the feel of the car. At least now she wouldn't have to rely on the bus and cabs to take her around.

Jill's parents arrived just before 4:00 and they insisted that, Katelyn join them for dinner, she objected at first insisting that they needed to spend time alone with Jill, but they wouldn't hear of it. They assured Katelyn that seeing Jill was a thrill of a lifetime, but it was also refreshing to know that Katelyn had gone out of her way to help Jill in the hour of need. Such diligence deserved at least a dinner out with them before they took their precious daughter home. Katelyn took her own car to the restaurant.

It was a wonderful experience to have dinner with the Bordens as they renewed their ties with Jill. Not once was it mentioned that she was foolish in not staying at home. The Bordens treated her as though she had just gone away to college and was returning home. After all, life's experience is like college. It prepares you for the future. Jill had apologized to her parents at Katelyn's apartment and that was all that was said about the whole affair. Katelyn sensed a deep bond between Jill and her parents, and she couldn't understand why Jill had run away from home in the first place.

After dinner, the Bordens thanked Kaitlyn again for befriending their daughter. Katelyn thanked them for the lovely dinner and told them that it had been a pleasure to help Jill out. Jill promised to write and let Katelyn know how she was getting on in life. She gave Katelyn her address in Calgary.

Since Jill's father was a bridge engineer, Katelyn thought it might be fun refreshing her memory of the building of the High Level Bridge. This bridge was the longest and highest of it's kind in the world, it would be worth checking out the history of the bridge once more.

Rolland and Katelyn had agreed about not seeing each other that evening, even though she was off, so that he could work on getting the contract done. Katelyn was proud of Rolland for his dedication to his work, so she didn't want to be a hindrance in Rolland achieving his own goal in life. He supported Katelyn in her dream, so the least she could do for him was to stand behind him while he climbed the ladder of success. Katelyn would just bury her nose in the building of the High Level Bridge.

Stopping of at the library before going home, she picked up the book by Alex Johnston, 'The C. P. Rail High Level Bridge at Lethbridge.' She had studied a bit about the building of the bridge in the past, but there was so much she had forgotten. It would be good to look at the bridges history again. Jill's dad had stirred up an interest within her to once again study the bridge in full detail.

At home, Katelyn got ready for bed and propping up her pillows, she read till midnight. There was so much interesting history in the book that it was hard to put it down. She realized how much she had forgotten once she began to read.

There were even things she had read before that seemed new to her as these things jumped off the page at her. It was phenomenal, all the effort that it took to erect the highest and longest bridge of it's kind in the world, right here in her own city. Katelyn was awe struck as she read the book and studied the pictures. She knew that reading this book once was not going to be enough, and it wouldn't do the book any justice.

The following day Katelyn got up earlier. She buried her nose in the book again and like always got lost in it's history, which was not surprising. Although the book was only forty pages long, Katelyn couldn't help admiring all the information that was written there. It also contained numerous pages of photos that were very intriguing. The thing that caught her attention was when she read about the accident that happened during the time the bridge was being built. A young man of twenty-one years of age met his death after falling two hundred ninety feet. His name was John Leslie Borden. Katelyn wondered if it was any relation to Jill's family. She would just have to write and ask. Maybe that was why her dad was a bridge engineer.

Since Rolland was still busy with the contract and it was Sunday, Kaitlyn didn't mind spending the day reading the history of the High Level Bridge, again. Everyone in the area seemed to take for granted that the bridge was there, so they never, or very seldom stopped to admire such a feat of architecture. Living in a place that had something that no other place in the world had, overwhelmed her. Although Katelyn wasn't romantically moved by what she had read, it still intrigued her to read the history behind this phenomenal undertaking. This bridge had been someone's dream, and it had taken almost three years to build. There had been much time put into it from the planning in 1906, till the time it had actually been finished in June of 1909.

When Katelyn put the book down, she was surprised that it was already bedtime. Rolland never even called her during the evening, so he must have been extremely busy with the account. She knew how important this job was for Rolland, and his boss was impressed with how well Rolland handled the accounts of clients assigned to him, and how he would take contracts home with him to work on over the weekend. Rolland was moving up the ladder of success very quickly.

Kaitlyn was so excited about finding out about John Leslie Borden, even after reading it again for the second or third time, that she decided to write to Jill right away the next morning and see if her dad could find out if there was a connection between them and John Leslie Borden. It would be interesting to see what her reply would be. History was a side of life that just had no end to it. Katelyn believed that everyone should take an interest in history, even though she knew that there were people who really could care less about what happened in the past. They only lived for today and tomorrow. She had tried to talk to a few elderly people about things that happened over the years, and they would only say that they wanted to forget the past. One old man had even said to her, "Let dead dogs lay." It didn't make sense why people wouldn't want to pass on the things that had taken place in their life, good or bad.

On the way to work the next day, Katelyn mailed the letter, because she wanted to get it out as quickly as possible. She had taken the High Level Bridge book with her, because even though she had read through the whole thing three times, it would still be exciting to look at the photos once more, if it was a slow night. It had been her experience that reading history more than once could prove to be very profitable in the end. Your mind never seemed to catch everything the first time around, so you could learn something new each time you read through a piece of history.

CHAPTER FOUR

AS THE DAYS PASSED by, and the weather grew warmer, Katelyn and Rolland spent many evenings on her days off walking in Indian Battle Park which in itself had a great history behind it. This was the place that the Blackfoot and Cree Nations fought a great battle back in the fall of 1870. The Blackfoot Indians chased the Crees right out of the country, after that bloody massacre that had happened right here in this park. She could almost hear the wild war cries of the Blackfoot and Cree Indians as they fought their last battle right there in the river bottom. Katelyn loved walking along the paths of yesteryear whenever she spent time in the Park. Coalbanks had started in the river bottom as well, when coal was first discovered by Nicholas Sheran. Many foundations of homes, and picket fences were the only suggestion that anything had been there before the bridge had been erected. Although there was much history surrounding Lethbridge, Katelyn still desired to work at the Victoria Museum.

One Thursday evening, Rolland had not been able to be with her on her time off because he had to drive to Calgary that morning for an important new client. Her days off were staggered and she didn't always have weekends off like Rolland did in his job. Since the motel was open twenty four seven, Katelyn had to take her turn working weekends. On this week, her days off happened to be Thursday and Friday. Sometimes her days off were split so she didn't always have two days off in a row. When she did get the weekend off, they made sure it was always a Saturday and Sunday together.

Katelyn had received a letter from Jill, and it was such a gorgeous evening out that she decided to take the letter down to the river bottom to read it. She took the car as far as the motel, and from there, she walked down the path into the park. Sitting at one of the pick nick tables, she proceeded to open the envelope. On the outside Jill had written, 'do not bend.' Once open, Katelyn retrieved the folded paper from inside, and as she unfolded the paper, a picture of Jill fell out. The picture looked so immaculate that Jill could pass as a model. Katelyn then read what Jill had to say.

To Katelyns surprise, Jill had written that the picture inclosed with the letter was of her modelling in a studio in Calgary. They were so impressed with Jill, that they were willing to train her to go on to bigger and better modelling positions. Along with her modelling, Jill had gone back to school to finish her high school education. Tears of joy rolled down Katelyn's cheeks, but she didn't bother to wipe them away. It was amazing how things could turn out, she thought as she pondered over what had transpired since meeting Jill as a vagabond. Katelyn was glad that she had lent Jill a listening ear that night, instead of turning her away. She was sure Jill would feel the same way.

As she read the rest of the letter, Jill had written that her dad was so excited about the information about John Leslie Borden, that he had checked out the family tree immediately to see if there was any connection. To his surprise, John Leslie had been the youngest brother of his grandfather. That would have made him Jill's great, uncle. According to the family tree, it all lined up with what Katelyn had read about John Leslie Borden falling to his death, two hundred ninety feet, on June 29, 1909. Sitting at the pick nick table, with a large tree branch overshadowing her, Katelyn thought about Jill making it big as a model. Jill sure had the beauty and the figure for it. Katelyn also reflected for a few moments on what she had studied about the High Level Bridge. She looked over from where she was sitting and admired the bridge afresh.

There sure was a lot of history behind Lethbridge, she thought as she let her mind drift off into the past. Maybe not as much as Victoria would have, but still enough for such a small city. Although she didn't attach any romantic story behind the bridge building, it was still a fascinating thing to just sit back and marvel over such a wonder. She could almost hear the sounds of the pneumatic rivetting hammers as they pounded the three hundred twenty eight thousand some odd rivets into the structure. It sent shivers of excitement up and down her spine as she could hear those sounds echoing throughout the river valley.

The sound of a train crossing the bridge brought her mind back to the present. Watching the train as it moved slowly along held her spellbound for a few minutes. It was very intriguing to think that the past one hundred years had seen many trains cross the river valley over this bridge. Katelyn wondered, how many people could actually say that they enjoyed sitting a spell while watching a train cross the valley floor high above their heads, on a steel structure that had been built between 1906 and 1909.

After the last car left the bridge, Katelyn sighed and put Jill's picture and the letter back into the envelope. Then she got up and move under one of the trees where she lay back to enjoy the shade. It wasn't long before Jill's letter was momentarily forgotten, and her thoughts were replaced with the sound of natives around the counsel fire. Even though the bridge had a great history behind it, she couldn't help thinking about the natives whenever she came to the park. Indian Battle Park had that kind of effect on her.

Small Pox had wiped out many of the people of this great nation known as Blackfoot, or "Tigers of the plains," as Mike Mountain Horse had written in his book, 'My People The Bloods.' The counsel members were concerned about what had happened to them, and it was evident that something had to be done in order to defeat this plague. The medicine men were at lose about what to do. Nothing they did seemed to work for them, and it looked as though the whole blackfoot nation would be destroyed by this deadly disease if something wasn't done quickly. Many of the old counsel members had been effected by small pox and died. The white man had brought this upon them, plus the fire water that made the Natives go so wild they fought among each other. Before the whites had come into this country, there was no such thing as small pox or fire water.

As Running Wild approached the counsel fire, the old man, who had been speaking, ceased and waited for him to pass by. Only the old men were able to sit around the counsel fire, because it was believed that over the years they had obtained great wisdom. The fact that they had reached an old age was proof that they had obtained the right to be part of the counsel. They had learned how to fight their enemies and win. Even the elements of nature had been unable to deprive them of that privilege. The only thing that stood in their way at this point was small pox. No young brave was allowed to participate unless he had been formerly invited to share about some great feat he had accomplished for the whole tribe.

Running Wild was a handsome brave who was nineteen summers old. He had already fought in many battles against the Cree, Sioux, Assiniboine, Crow and Kutenia. Now that there was talk about the plague that was destroying the Blackfoot Nation, Running Wild wanted to know more about the plans of the counsel men. He knew the rules about the young braves not being allowed in the counsel circle, but he had to try. It was his opinion that to many of these old men were more like old women, that they needed more young blood speaking at the counsel fires, to awaken the old ways of fighting back. All that the old men seemed to be interested in was to make peace with the white man and to live together in harmony. Everyone of the tribe members knew that Running Wild was very ambitious and that he feared no one. They also knew that he was pushing to get the young braves to speak in favour of having young and old alike at the counsel fires, but so far he was standing alone. It was a well known fact, that among the young and old alike, Running Wild was highly regarded, yet without any say in tribal matters.

Pretty Bird, the beautiful daughter of "Many Scars", the well respected Shaman of the Blackfoot, stood in the doorway of her mothers teepee watching as Running Wild approached the counsel fire. She was sixteen summers old, and she admired Running Wild for being so persistent. Her father would be upset, because Running Wild once more insisted on disturbing the gathering of the tribal fathers. Many Scars, knew what it meant to earn your way into the counsel circle. Over the years, he had fought many battles against their enemies. Through all the wars, which started long before he married Gentle Woman, Many Scars suffered a great deal of knife and arrow wounds, plus a spear wound to his mid section, while learning the art of fighting and staying alive. Thus he had earned the name Many Scars. Gentle woman had always been there when she was just a young girl, and had tended to his wounds until he was strong enough to do battle again. Through her gentle way of treating his wounds, she had received the name Gentle Woman. They eventually married, and due to complications, were only given one child, Pretty Bird.

Although Pretty Birds heart yearned to have Running Wild take her as his wife, she also knew that the other girls of the tribe felt the same way about Running Wild as she did, and it angered her a bit. She wanted him all to herself, but for some strange reason, he hadn't noticed her. At least he didn't let on that he had noticed her, but then, he didn't seem to notice any of the young girls in the tribe. She would be a good wife to Running Wild, Pretty Bird had convinced herself, bearing him many strong warrior sons, and beautiful daughters. Why didn't the Great Spirit grant her this wish.

While she dreamed on, Chief Red Crow spoke to Running Wild with authority, "Running Wild, you know that you are still to young to attend these counsel meetings."

"I know, Great Chief," Running Wild insisted, "But it is important for our tribes survival that we have young blood at the fires."

"I understand how you feel about these things and so do all the old men of the counsel," the Chief continued, "It has been our custom since the time of the old ones before us to let the old and wise make the decisions for each and everyone of us, and so it will continue for as long as the Blackfoot nation remains on the earth."

"So many of the elders have died because of this deadly plague the white man has brought upon us," Running Wild argued. "I believe that it is a mistake not to have the young warriors join in to learn before it is too late."

"I appreciate your concern," Red Crow acknowledged, "But as long as there are elders to seek counsel from, only they will be allowed to attend counsel fire meetings. As long as we have Shaman like Many Scars, they will seek direction from the Great Spirit as to what is to come."

"But if the old men all die from this dreaded disease," Running Wild persisted, "Who will have taught the young braves how to counsel?"

Seeing the hopelessness to pursue the issue any further, Running Wild turned to go when Red Crow stopped him. "Running Wild, you are a very good and brave warrior, and I know that when the time comes for you to sit at the counsel fires, your wisdom will be greatly appreciated."

Running Wild grunted in response, and then without another word, headed for his own mothers teepee. He was so angry with the old men at the counsel fire, that he didn't even notice Pretty Bird watching him as he storm by. She wanted to speak out to him, but she knew that this was not the proper thing to do. A girl was not suppose to throw herself at a brave, no matter how strong her love for him may be. First the brave must notice her, and show signs of interest in her, then she could go to him at his beckoning. While her breasts heaved with desire to be near him, her heart was pounding so hard, she was surprised that it didn't leap out of her body. There had to be a way to attract his attention, and get his mind off of becoming the greatest warrior that ever fought in Blackfoot battles. She pictured herself in his arms just before he would go out to war against the enemy, encouraging him, and then praying to the Great Spirit to protect him and bring him home again with many scalps to his name. She would sit in her teepee and cause the smoke from sweet grass to fill the air, as she fanned the savouring smoke all over her body to purify it.

Why couldn't he even notice her? It angered Pretty Bird just a little to think that Running Wild must know that she existed. Why then was he ignoring her? Other braves had noticed her, even asking her to become their wife. She had flatly refused them, because her heart was set on marrying Running Wild.

Pretty Bird went back into her mothers teepee and sat glumly by the fire. Gentle Woman, came and sat by her side. She knew how Pretty Bird felt about Running Wild, and she had watched from inside the teepee as Pretty Bird kept her eyes on him as he had approached the counsel fire. She was a good woman, and she knew that it was her responsibility to make sure that her daughter and husband were cared for. This was not the first time Pretty Bird needed a comforting arm of support around her. Since Gentle Woman was only able to give Many Scars one child, he had the right to take to himself another wife, but Many Scars had love for only one woman, and this caused Gentle Woman to work even harder to make her warrior brave, a happy man.

Gentle Woman remembered to well how she had yearned to be in the arms of Many Scars, and how she had gone against tribal rule by reaching out to him before he noticed her, and caring for him, whenever he came back wounded from battle. Even Chief Black Bear, Red

Crows father, had not scolded her when he recognized the deep devotion she had toward Many Scars. Black Bear was a very wise Chief knowing a good thing when he saw it. Many Scars had recognized this trait in her, and had taken her to be his wife. Today she would try to console her daughter in her time of need.

"My child," she spoke softly to Pretty Bird, "Stop trying so hard."

"But mother," Pretty Bird insisted, "Why can't he even acknowledge that I am alive?"

"Right now my child," Gentle Woman continued, "Running Wild is to busy making a name for himself. He is a very aggressive brave, and he has decided that he will be part of the counsel fire meetings at a young age. I doubt that he even notices any girls at this time."

"That is foolish thinking on his part mother," Pretty Bird was almost in tears. "I'll be an old woman before he takes me to be his wife, if he even notices me. He might even get himself killed before I have the opportunity to make him happy."

"Now, now my child," Gentle Woman hugged Pretty Bird, "You must not think that way. The Great Spirit will direct your footsteps, and you must obey what he wants from you."

"I know that is true mother, but that doesn't change the feelings I have for Running Wild." Pretty Bird began to cry.

"Leave him in the hands of the Great Spirit," Gentle Woman whispered as she placed a kiss on her daughters forehead.

Gentle Woman rocked her daughter back and forth, as Pretty Birds tears streamed down her cheeks. Pretty Bird would become the wife of some brave in good time. Whether it was Running Wild, or some other brave, but right now she was infatuated with being Running Wilds wife. Then again, so were most of the young girls in the tribe. She thought of how she had been afraid of losing Many Scars to someone else, and how she had gone against the rules, by mending his wounds whenever he came back from battle. That time he had been pierced in the mid section with a spear, she had spent many moons looking after him, fearful that she would lose him every time a fever broke out. Now would be a good time to tell her daughter that part of her life. Pretty Bird was so much like she had been as a young girl.

When she was done telling Pretty Bird how she had won her fathers admiration, she also told her that Red Crow might not look at things the way his father Black Bear had viewed things. Red Crow had become Chief only a short while ago, after his father had died. Although he had made a name for himself, and had the respect of his people, he had not yet been chief long enough for the people to know which way he was going to lead them. The white man had come into the country and built a Fort, which the Blackfoot had burnt to the ground, but they already built another Fort, and this time the natives were trading with them, buffalo hides for firewater. The firewater was destroying the Blackfoot nation, along with the dreaded disease, small pox. Red Crow, along with the elders were concerned about the outcome of this dreaded disease. Red Crow realized that it was no use fighting the white man, because they would just keep coming. After burning the first Fort, named after the man they called Hamilton, they just came and rebuilt another Fort which they called Fort-Whoop-Up. Then his people got hooked on the white man's firewater, and they started fighting among themselves, even killing one another. Although he wanted to put a stop to his people trading furs and skins for fire water, Red Crow also knew that other things that were traded for the skins, had great use. Most of his people had become obsessed by what fire water made them feel like.

Then there was this matter of Running Wild insisting that young braves should be allowed to sit around the counsel fires. He had valid reasons for the young to participate and learn from the old men, who were dying off, as small pox ravaged their Nation. The Medicine Men were helpless in what to do, because in the face of this dreaded disease, they had no power to chase it away. The Shaman, like Many Scars, had no answer from the Great Spirit. Life had been much less complicated before the white man came on the scene.

"Katelyn," somewhere between reality and dream land, Katelyn wasn't sure if she heard her name, or if Running Wild was calling to Pretty Bird. Her heart just melted at the thought of Running Wild noticing her. Maybe now he would take her to be his wife.

"Katelyn," there it was again. But wait, that was not "Pretty Bird" that she heard. It was, "Katelyn, and it sounded like Rolland calling to her from some far off place.

"Katelyn Sweety, wake up."

Katelyn smiled as she realized that she was only dreaming. Rolland was in Calgary and she wouldn't see him until tomorrow. The imagination sure is a wonderfully strange thing she thought to herself. She was deep in thought about the natives that roamed this land long before the white man ever came, and through it all, she imagined Rolland calling out to her.

"Katelyn Sweety, I'm home. What are you smiling about?" Rollands voice came through the fog in her imagination.

Opening her eyes, she was surprised to see Rolland kneeling down beside her, looking directly into her face. Was this just another dream, or was it for real, she wondered.

Reaching up, she brushed her hand across his face, and then reality set in. Rolland was here beside her in Indian Battle Park. It was true, but yet the reality of it all didn't seem to want to click with her. Rolland was in Calgary, so how could he be here with her as well. Had she fallen asleep and slept in the park over night? She blinked her eyes and shock her head, but the image of Rolland before her wouldn't leave.

"Honey, is that really you?" Katelyn whispered, for fear that this illusion would fade away leaving her depressed as her mind cleared.

"Yes Sweety," Rolland laughed at her."Who else could I be? Has your dreaming about the past got your brain a bit foggy?"

Katelyn was fully aware by now that this was not a dream. Rolland really was here with her, but it puzzled her, because he was not suppose to be back home till the next day.

"How is it that you are home so soon?" she questioned him.

"I couldn't bear to be without you," Rolland laughed at the weird expression on Katelyn's face.

"But your meeting was going to last till late tonight," Katelyn insisted.

"I could go back if you want me too," Rolland teased her.

"Don't you dare!" Katelyn grabbed a hold of him, pulling him down beside her. There was no way she would let go of Rolland now that he was back home. Running

Wild didn't know what he was missing by ignoring Pretty Bird.

"Well Sweety," Rolland smiled at her as they faced each other on the ground. "I got to Calgary this morning, only to find out that just moments before arriving at their office, the boss got called away, so they postponed till next week sometime. Now, what was it that had you so intrigued that I had to call you from some other time and place?"

Katelyn told him a bit of what she had been thinking about. Of course, she left out the part about Running Wild and Pretty Bird. He only needed to know that she was thinking about the way things were before the white man entered the picture.

Talking to Rolland about how it must have been back then, she thought of what the country must have looked like. They talked about there being no roads, and bridges for the Indians to cross over on. They would have to ford the river where the water was shallow. Katelyn had read about the men doing the hunting and fishing, while the women tended to the worked around the camp making sure that there was food to eat when the men came back. The grandparents would watch the children. While grandfathers told stories and passed on legends, grandmothers would make sure the children were listening.

Their teepee's were made by wrapping hides around large poles, leaving an opening at the top for smoke to escape through. A flap was placed over the entrance to act as a door. These teepee's would be warm in the winter, and cool in the summer. They could also withstand very rough weather. The teepee's belonged to the woman, so the men would have to get permission from the women if they wanted to decorate the teepee.

Katelyn wondered what it would have been like being a native woman back then, working hard at preparing and curing fresh hides to be used in making moccasins and clothing. In her dream world, she had thought wonderful thoughts about Running Wild and Pretty Bird but, did they have the same romantic feelings like she had towards Rolland? Was she only thinking these thoughts about Running Wild and Pretty Bird because of her feelings for the man she so deeply desired to have. She couldn't imagine it, but she knew there must have been some feelings to draw them together. It sure wasn't candle light dinners that set their evenings off. Then again, maybe it would be romantic sitting around a fire in a teepee looking longingly at the man you loved, sitting across the fire from you.

She pictured Pretty Bird serving Running Wild his evening meal in the teepee. After he received his food, she retreated to the other side of the fire, where she sat down across from him. It was with loving admiration that she looked over at Running Wild and watched as he devoured the meal she had prepared for him. He ate with pleasure, showing his gratitude with occasional grunts which he utered between mouthfuls. When he was done his meal, she would eat hers.

Whenever Katelyn got into her dreaming mode, Rolland would wait patiently for her to return to reality. He knew that she needed to live these times in order to fulfil the desire in her heart. Just to be near Katelyn made up for the times that she quietly dreamed of by-gone days. As long as he could hold her hand and be by her side, that was all it took to make his body temperature rise to an almost uncontrollable level.

Katelyn looked at Rolland from where they were still laying on the ground facing each other. The man sure had to be patient to be going out with someone like her. She was always off somewhere else, and Rolland never discouraged her from having her dreams. His carrier as accountant kept his mind filled with numbers and figures of accounts he dealt with so he just thought on those things while Katelyn travelled around in her dream world.

"I think we should go and have something to drink," Katelyn spoke lovingly to Rolland. "Then after that, you may take me home."

"You mean that you want to come to my place tonight," Rolland teased.

"Oh! You silly man," Katelyn scolded playfully. "You know exactly what I mean."

"Didn't you bring your own car?" Rolland questioned.

"Oh ya!" Katelyn exclaimed. "How silly of me. I left it at the motel and walked down here."

"So I can't take you to my place then?" Rolland continued to tease.

"For your own good, and mine," Katelyn laughed at him, "I think that you should go to your home, and I'll go to my apartment."

"How about we go for coffee somewhere first." Rolland chided as he got up off the ground.

"I like that very much," Katelyn answered.

Rolland helped Katelyn to her feet and then she taunted him to come catch her. As she ran out into the tall grass in the open field, Rolland went after her. Katelyn was laughing so hard that she fell headlong into the tall grass, and Rolland dropped down beside her. Wrapping his arms around her, he kissed her and jumped to his feet. He reached out his hand and once more pulled Katelyn up off the ground. This time he didn't let go of her hand, because this time she was not going to make him chase her. As they headed for the car, Katelyn chuckled about how she had tried to run from Rolland, only to trip and fall. It felt good to have his arms around her in loving embrace, as they had laid on the ground together momentarily.

While they drove out of the river bottom, Katelyn let Rolland know that she was happy about him coming back from Calgary and surprising her in Indian Battle Park. Although she knew that some down time apart from each other was good, she still relished the idea of having Rolland by her side. If only he would propose to her, then they could be together all the time. She sighed out loud and Rolland turned to look over at her.

"What is it Sweetie?"

"Oh, I was just thinking about how nice it is to have you here instead of in Calgary," Katelyn sighed again.

"But you know that I have to go away sometimes," Rolland insisted.

"I know Honey," Katelyn placed her hand on his arm, "It's just so much nicer to have you here by my side."

"You realize that as the firm grows, I might be asked to go away for two days to a week from time to time," Rolland interjected.

"I understand," Katelyn sighed, "But that doesn't mean I have to like it."

Rolland laughed, "Honey, I am happy that you miss me while I'm gone, because I can hardly wait to get back to you when I leave. In fact I start missing you already before I leave."

Katelyn squeezed his arm as she silently sat by and admired the man she cherished with all her heart. She couldn't help but wonder how the native women must have felt as their warriors rode off on hunts or to fight with their enemies. They would truly have to put their trust in the Great Spirit to bring their men back safely. Of course, if they didn't return, they were praised for their bravery.

Rolland just smiled as he drove over to Humpty's Family Restaurant. He knew how Katelyn felt about him, and he wished that he could propose to her, but he respected her dream. While they enjoyed a soft drink together, Katelyn told him about Jill's letter, and showed her picture to him. Rolland was tired from his trip to and from Calgary, so they didn't stay in Humpty's to long, and after he drove her back to her car, Katelyn assured him that it was okay that he was tired. She would just entertain herself by burying her nose into a good history book, or dream.

Instead of driving home, Katelyn decided to drive back down into Indian Battle Park. She desired to think a bit more on the History of the Blackfoot nation from by gone days, and since this was her evening off, she had nothing better to do then to dream. Parking the car in the parking area, near the first pick nick shelter, she ventured back over to where Rolland had caught her dreaming before. As she lay down under the old Cottonwood tree, she closed her eyes with the hopes that her dream about Pretty Bird and Running Wild would continue. Her mind went back to the counsel fire scene, but the fire was now only ambers, and nobody was sitting there. Everyone had gone to sleep.

Suddenly, the camp was awakened by the sound of a hysterical woman. "Mountain Chiefs camp is being attacked by the Cree Nation," she cried out.

The whole Blood Tribe, ruled by Red Crow, was alerted and soon the brave Blackfoot warriors were mounted upon their horses and ready to ride into battle. A messenger was sent to the Peigans and they made ready to aid the Blood Tribe in defending their Blackfoot brothers being attacked. Running Wild had been one of the first warriors to get mounted, after the news came and he was anxious to ride. They had fought the Cree on numerous occasions before, but that was always during daylight hours. It was strange that they would attack at night, and they were attacking Mountain Chief's small camp.

The sound of rife fire and the barking of dogs, could be heard for miles. Soon there were Blackfoot Indians riding abreast in twos or threes over every hill and down into the Valley, shouting and shrieking their battle cry, taking the Crees by surprise. Although it was hard to fight in the dark, the Blackfoot all but annihilated that group of Crees. They drove them into the river, and with all the blood, the water turned red. Very few Blackfoot lost their lives that night, and they returned back to their own camps, the Pikanii(Piegan), Kainai(Bloods), and Siksika(Blackfoot), all members of the Blackfoot Nation, and yet tribes of their own. They were known all over as the "Tigers of the Plains." Another successful battle was credited to that name, that night in the late fall of 1870.

As the braves returned to their own teepee, Pretty Bird waited outside her mother's teepee. Her father appeared out of the dark, along with all the other braves that made it back through the battle alive. As she watched, she did not see Running Wild, but then it was hard to tell in the dark who made it and who didn't. Pretty Bird snuck off into the night, and headed for Running Wild's mother's teepee, to wait and see his return. She stayed well hidden in the dark, because she knew it wasn't proper for a women to be chasing after a young brave. Only the mothers and wives of the braves would attend to the wounded. After all the braves had returned, Running Wild was not among them. It had been decided that when the Sun came up, then they could go in search of the dead, and bury them proper, so that their spirit could rest in peace. The Crees were gone, so they could not steal the dead bodies, to cause those spirits to roam the earth without rest. The spirits of the dead Crees would never find rest but would roam around in eternal darkness, because their people were not there to properly bury them.

Pretty Bird felt that Running Wild was not dead, and that he was laying out in the dark somewhere, hurt and unable to return to camp without proper help. Without a word to anyone, she quietly got a horse ready to ride out to where the battle had taken place. She knew it was dangerous, because there was the chance that a Cree might be lying out there wounded as well, and if she ran into him, he would kill her, but she must find Running Wild, dead or alive. Leading the horse far enough away from camp that no one would hear it leave, she leaped to it's back and made a hasty retreat to the battle ground. The sky was overcast with thunderclouds so even the light from the moon was obscured. It was dangerous riding in the dark, but Pretty Bird was persistent in finding Running Wild before morning, if he was not dead but wounded. Fear gripped her heart as she slowly let the horse find its own footing. One slip from the horse could be fatal to her own self as she spilled out on the ground in the darkness.

She arrived at the battle ground, and for a couple hours Pretty Bird search in vain, calling Running Wild's name quietly every now again. She proceeded to check every tree, gully, and notch in the ground, finding many bodies laying around. They were mostly Cree, and a few Blackfoot, but she was not successful in finding Running Wild among the dead. It was an eerie feeling to be walking among the dead in the darkness. Every now and again a clap of thunder would terrify Pretty Bird, but no rain came. By morning the clouds were dissipating and the sun was coming up in the eastern sky. Pretty

Bird was exhausted from the search, and she knew that it was not good to be found out there when the men from the Blackfoot camps returned for the dead, but she just couldn't give up. She needed to find Running Wild's body, although she felt strongly that he was laying out there wounded but still alive. She decided to search for a few more minutes before leaving the battle ground. In hopelessness, she finally headed back to where she had tied up the horse. It was then that she heard a moan and a slight russel in a bush nearby. Approaching cautiously, she pulled back the branches to find that it was Running Wild, and he had a bullet wound in the chest, and a knife wound to the mid section. He had lost a lot of blood, and was badly in need of proper care.

Remembering what her mother had told her about taking care of her father, Pretty Bird set about the task of binding up Running Wild's wounds the best she could. If she was found by the party returning for the dead, she would just take what punishment came to her. It was her hopes that Running Wild would remember what she had done for him, and that then she could become his wife.

Pretty Bird spoke reassuringly to him about the battle being won, and that he was wounded, and badly in need of rest. Although the task was dificult, Pretty Bird worked hard and got the wounds wrapped up. She could feel he was running a high fever, and he kept mumbling things that made no sense. The loss of blood and the fever, were causing him to hallucinate, not even knowing where he was. He mumbled something about ridding the land of the Crees, once and for all. She worked frantically, yet gently to get Running Wild able to sit on the horse.

Finally the job was completed, but not before the party of warriors returned to retrieve the dead bodies. Upon seeing her, Many Scars admonished her for being out this far away from camp. Secretly he admired her for what she had done. 'Just like her mother,' he thought, but for the benefit of the rest of the party, he spoke in an authoritative voice, "Pretty Bird, what are you doing out here by yourself? You know it is forbidden for you to be out looking for survivors in the dark. There are evil spirits roaming around in the dark hours. You have been a very foolish child."

"I am sorry Father," Pretty Bird began to weep. "I felt in my heart that Running Wild was still alive, and I just needed to come find out for myself."

"You know that had he died out here because of his wounds, he would have entered into the happy hunting grounds."

Many Scars tried hard to scold his daughter, but yet admired her for her bravery in searching for Running Wild alone in the dark. The blood of her mother truly ran in her veins, but Many Scars felt in his heart that there was much more to his daughter then being just a young woman in love. He believed that the true blood of a Shaman also ran through her veins, and that the Great Spirit was tugging at her heart. He believed that the powers of darkness and the Great Spirit were at war for her soul. For her it was dangerous to be walking around in the dark alone, especially out on a battle field where a war had been fought in the night. The spirit of death could enter into her and cause many problems during her life. Death would be walking with her every step of the way trying to kill her.

Many Scars looked at his daughter and saw the tears as she spoke. "I know I've done wrong Father, but please don't tell Chief Red Crow what I did," Pretty Bird looked at her father with pleadings for his approval.

"You go home now," Many Scars commanded, "I will deal with you later."

Mounting her horse, Pretty Bird rode past her father, who patted her arm, without the others seeing it, to show his approval of what she had done, even though it still concerned him. She smiled as she headed for camp, because she believed strongly that her father remembered how her mother had watched over him while he lay suffering on his bed. She believed that her mother had already let Many Scars know how Pretty Bird felt about Running Wild. She also knew about the dangers of her being out alone in the dark with spirits lurking around, but she didn't believe that she was in any danger of these spirits entering her. After all, wasn't the power of the Great Spirit more superior then that of evil spirits. Then what had she to be afraid of. Yes, she had gone against the rules of the Blackfoot Nation by going out alone in the dark, but it had been for a good cause. She was convinced that the Great Spirit had protected her from evil because of the good she was set on doing. After all, her father had always taught her that the Great Spirit was all powerful.

Although Many Scars did not like the way Running Wild kept insisting on barging in on their counsel fire meetings, at the same time he secretly admired Running Wild for his persistence. His daughter had chosen well the man she wanted for her lifetime partner, but the question still remained. Is this what the Great Spirit wanted for her? Not only was Running Wild persistent in disturbing counsel fire meetings, he was just as persistent in battles against the enemy. A smile crossed Many Scars face as he watched his daughter riding away. If need be, he would talk with Chief Red Crow not to go hard on her, after all, Black Bear had allowed her mother to stay by Many Scars side as he healed. As well, Many Scars had deep desires to take his daughter to visit the place where before the Blackfoot time, the ancient ones had written their stories on the walls of the cliffs at a place where the sun came up every morning. He wanted his daughter to remember the ways of her people, since he had learned in his travelling days, the white man was fighting hard to rid them of their native ways. The white man was calling the natives, savages, but Many Scars often wondered who the real savages were. How could one race of people demand another race to neglect the teachings of the old ones. Maybe his daughter would desire a Vision Quest while they were at the sacred place of the writings on the wall.

Katelyn came out of her dream world to realize that the sun was going down and she should go home. She could always come back to dream another day. As she headed for her car, she couldn't help smiling to herself, because her imagination sure made for an interesting life. She liked dreaming about Pretty Bird, and could only hope that her dream would have a happy ending. If only Rolland would propose to her, then she could match up Pretty Bird and Running Wild as well, but in the mean time, she could only dream about Pretty Bird's desire to have Running Wild, just like Katelyn's deep burning desire to be married to Rolland. As she thought about Rolland, she couldn't help but think of Rose, in the movie Titanic, and the one night relationship she had with Jack before she lost him forever. Even though she had secretly carried in her heart, the memory of Jack all her life, Katelyn couldn't help imagine what it must have been like to be intimate with Jack and then have tragedy strike.

"Stop thinking like that," Katelyn scolded herself out loud, but she couldn't help feeling the way she did about Rolland. Had it been a mistake for them to have gone to see Titanic? It seemed that ever since that movie, Katelyn's desire to be intimate with Rolland had grown stronger. If only the man would propose, they could get married, and merge into eternal bliss.

Driving home, Katelyn thought about the battle that had been fought in Indian Battle Park. It had been the last battle to take place between the two native tribes. She thought about Mountain Chief, who's tribe had been attacked by the Crees, before the whole Blackfoot Confederacy had come to their aid.

She remembered reading about Mountain Chief somewhere else in the history of the Blackfoot Nation.

She would just have to get on the computer and surf the net for information on Mountain Chief.

At home, Katelyn got on the computer with all intentions of only spending a few minutes downloading the information she wanted, and then she would go to bed. Of course, once she got into the history behind Mountain Chief, she couldn't stop checking further, and got into the Marias River Massacre, led by Major Eugene Baker, 2nd U.S. Cavalry, Fort Ellis, Montana. Katelyn was appalled at what she read. The useless butchering of innocent natives, because some Major and his cavalry were to drunk to think straight, and their hatred for Natives made them irrational.

Although the Marias River Massacre was not a romantic scene, Katelyn couldn't help dreaming about that incident. She could already see it unfolding in her mind. Major Baker was summoned into General Sheridan's office, as he had come to Fort Ellis with a very important mission.

As Major Eugene Baker entered the office that cold day on January 15th 1870, General Sheridan motioned him to sit down in one of the two chairs in front of the desk. There had been some complaints about the Blackfoot Indians stealing horses from the local Ranchers near Browning. The main group was led by Mountain Chief, and it was important that they be stopped and punished by death as a lesson to all other Native tribes.

"Major," the General looked directly at Baker as he spoke, "I want you to take two hundred of the best officers here at Fort Ellis, and I want you to march to Mountain Chiefs camp and destroy it."

"I will get right on it Sir," Baker replied.

"Here is the document ordering you to destroy the camp, and take as many prisoners as you can." The General held out the paper on which he had authorized Baker to go after and retrieve the horses that had been stolen, at the same time punishing the natives for stealing horses, and destroying property that belonged to someone else.

Major Baker left the office and started barking orders, "Lieutenant Doane, I want you to round up two hundred of our best cavalry men to go fight some Indians."

"Yes Sir Major," Doane saluted Baker.

"And Lieutenant," Baker's voice stopped Doane in his tracks.

"Yes Sir Major?" Doane turned around and faced Baker.

"Tell the men to dress warm and take extra clothing, because there will be no fires as we proceed towards Mountain Chiefs camp."

"Yes Sir," Doane Saluted Baker again.

"Tell the men we are leaving immediately, on the double."

"Understood Sir." Doane turned to inform the men of the plan.

As he entered the barracks, Lieutenant Doane knew how the men would feel about a forced march of seven or eight days, in the bitter winter cold. The weather had been between thirty and forty degrees below zero for the past two or three weeks. Then to have to travel over land for that distance without a fire to warm up by and to eat cold meals all the while, Doane knew the men would not be thrilled.

When the party of two hundred officers was prepared and ready to march. Baker explained to the men that the reason for no fires, was so that the Indians would not know they were coming. Joe Kipp, an army scout, would lead the way, because apparently he knew where the camp was located. For days, the troop rode their horses into the bitter cold. At night they huddled as close together as they could to try and stay warm from body heat. They drank hard liquor to try and warm up their blood, but after a couple days, the cold and the liquor was taking it's toll on the men. Baker had to keep reminding the men that they were on a mission, and that when they got there, each man could shot as many Indians that his heart desired to shot.

"Men," Baker would say each day, "Remember this, the only good Indian is a dead Indian."

The mens spirits would be lifted for a while, as each man realized that shooting these Indians would be a free for all. The life in the cavalry had taught these men to hate the Indian, and some of the men had lost family members through Indian attacks. Other members of the cavalry had families who lost livestock, especially horses to the native people. Taking horses from another tribe was something that the Natives had done long before the white man started ranching and farming in this country. The Spanish had brought horses over hundreds of years earlier. For these natives, ranches were easy targets for horse thieving. In the white mans eyes, stealing a horse meant the thief was punished by death. The men of the cavalry understood to well what stealing a horse meant. The natives not only stole one horse, but they stole many, thus these men were all fired up to kill themselves some

Indians. The fact that they were getting liquored up everyday, didn't help either. The weather might have been cold, but they were going to do a job, which to most of these men, and especially Major Eugene Baker, was going to be satisfactory. Baker hated the natives with a passion, and it showed in his attitude.

On January 22, the two hundred man cavalry arrive near Marias River, where the Blackfoot Tribe was supposed to be camped for the winter. The Buffalo were plentiful in the valley, so this was a great winter camp for the natives. The men had orders to dismount and rest till night fall. They would continue on to the camp by night so that they would not be detected. By morning, they reached the bluffs overlooking the Indian camp. Since the sun was just starting to come up, there was very little movement in the camp at that time. One native was leading his horse to the edge of camp. It looked like he was about to go hunting. As he walked his horse, he happened to look towards the bluffs, and his eye caught some movement up top. Focussing his eyes on the spot where the movement had come from, he noticed first one blue coat, and then another, and another. He dropped the halter rope that held the horse, and he went running through the camp announcing that the blue coats were coming.

At all the commotion, Heavy Runner, Chief of the group, came running out of the teepee, holding up his papers and medals, showing that he was friendly with the white man. Joe Kipp shouted at Baker that this was the wrong camp, but Baker was not interested. These were Indians, and his hate for them didn't matter if it was the wrong camp or not.

"Kipp," Baker barked at him, "I am warning you to shut your mouth, or suffer the consequences."

"This is not the right camp," Kipp was angry with Lieutenant Baker. "I insist you turn away from this camp, because this is Heavy Runner's camp, and not the camp of Mountain Chief."

A shot rang out, and as Kipp turned to look, he saw Heavy Runner crumple to the ground. Then there was a barrage of gunfire, and natives were dropping everywhere. Kipp's anger towards Lieutenant Baker mounted for not listening to the truth and for Baker's hatred towards the red man. The cavalry stormed the camp and rounded up the women and children, and Kipp busied himself counting the dead. Some of the cavalry men were ordered to round up the horses. It was a horrible day to remember, as the cavalry picked up the dead bodies and just dumped them on top of the collapsed lodges that were on fire.

They had no respect for the dead, and this angered Kipp even more. He swore that someday he would reveal what had really happened here on January 23rd 1870.

The cavalry moved out and headed for Mountain Chief's camp a few miles down river. When they got there, the camp was cleared out, and from the look of the camp, they had cleared out in a hurry. There were tracks in the snow leading in every direction. It would be difficult rounding up Mountain Chief's tribe, so the cavalry took their prisoners and the horses and headed back to Fort Ellis.

There was so much to read on the internet about the Marias River massacre, with one section reporting fifteen testimonies from different people who had been there. There were officers that gave testimony, plus natives who also testified about what Lieutenant Baker had done. Even the Scout, Joe Kipp testified as he had promised, but these testimonies all came years after it had happened. Katelyn found nowhere in the history of the massacre that Lieutenant Eugene Baker ever got charged for his misconduct and slaughter of innocent people. Baker had just stated that the killing of the Heavy Runner camp would teach other Indians that Heavy Runner and all the others were killed in payment for any sins the natives did or would do in the future.

Katelyn was angry when she was done studying about the Marias River massacre. She realized that the white man were so in debt to the natives, as well as the African Americans, that they would never be able to pay for what they had done to them. It made no sense how the white man could think they were better than any other race or colour. The natives had a unique way of life before the white man entered the picture. Every culture had their own way of doing things, and that did not mean that one culture was greater than the next. All cultures should be able to work together for one cause, and that was for the survival of mankind.

Looking at the clock, Katelyn realized she had been so involved with native history, she hadn't even thought about going to bed. It was already nearly one o'clock in the morning, so she decided to try and shut her mind off till the next day.

Rolland called in the morning to let Katelyn know that the firm was sending him back to Calgary and putting him up in a hotel so he could meet with the new client that day, and if need be, also on Saturday morning. They figured he'd be gone at least two days because the account was bigger than what they had first anticipated. Mr. Wheeland, the company owner, had apologized about the meeting he was called to the day before, but assured the firm he would be willing to pay handsomely for the accountant driving up and back for nothing. Mr. Wheeland was looking forward to meeting with Rolland and changing accountants because of the great report he had heard from other Calgary businesses associated with the Firm.

Since Katelyn was intrigued by what she had learned the night before, she surfed the internet on the topic of massacres, and came across the Sand Creek Massacre. Although she hated what the whites had done to other cultures, Katelyn couldn't help studying more history on that subject. One thing about it, she could not dream of Rolland through out these studies. Rolland could never be as cruel as these men had been.

The Cheyenne and Arapaho were attacking wagon trains, mining camps, and stage coach lines together. The Civil War was raging in the east and the natives were trying hard to discourage the whites from coming west. Gold fever was in the white mans blood and everyone desired a piece of the action. The coming of the white man had caused the natives to have less land to hunt on.

Governor John Evans had decided to do something about the native uprising. Under the command of Colonel John Chivington they managed to gather up about seven hundred volunteer militia men to wage war against the Cheyenne and Arapahos. Colonel Chivington had been a pastor in the Methodist denomination, but his compassion for his fellow man didn't extend to the natives. He wanted to see all natives annihilated from the earth.

Black Kettle, the chief of a band of about six hundred Cheyenne and Arapaho, reported to Fort Lyon to let them know they were a peaceful band. They set up camp on Sand Creek, about forty miles from the Fort, where they would be under the protection of the United States government and their army. Black Kettle had seen, in his lifetime, the continuous flow of whites coming into the country. He knew it was hopeless to fight against them because they would keep sending bigger and bigger armies to defeat the natives. It was his desire to live in peace with the white man and to try and work something out with this greedy race of people.

When Colonel Chivington arrived at Fort Lyon he was informed that Black Kettle's band of natives was not to be harmed because they had already surrendered. Chivington was tired of hunting the natives responsible for the uprising, and his army of volunteers had searched hard for the renegades, but came up empty handed. It angered Colonel Chivington that natives were now being protected, when in his mind, all natives should be annihilated. He made up his mind that they would ignore that Black Kettle was at peace with the whites. They would just ride down there and exterminate every native in the camp. Chivington laughed as he thought about how easy it would be to attack the unsuspecting Black Kettle camp. He had no plans of taking prisoners because that would defeat his desire to see all natives wiped of the face of the earth.

Chivington discussed his plan with a couple Sergeants, and although they argued the fact that Black Kettle was under government protection, they could see the purpose for such an attack. The Colonel told them that if the peaceful ones were exterminated, they could no longer breed more of their kind who might grow up wanting to fight back.

"We will cut those red devils to pieces where they stand, and with the use of our four howitzers we can destroy that whole camp before they know what hit them," Chivington told his sergeants.

"You would even kill the children!" one sergeant spoke out, appalled at what he heard the Colonel saying.

Colonel Chivington glared at the sergeant, and then spit out vehemently, "Nits make lice."

They moved out and worked their way to Black Kettle's camp, and when Black Kettle saw the army approaching, he quickly raised up the American flag and a white flag to show that they were peaceful. As the flags rose above Chief Black Kettle's teepee, Colonel Chivington gave the order for attack. Unprepared for what came upon them, the camp was filled with screams and desperate cries of woman and children as the braves scurried about trying to get their bows and arrows into action. Women, who's bellies were ripped open with the white man's sharp knives, screamed as their insides gushed out onto the ground. Little children wailed as the troopers literally smashed their heads in with the butt of their rifles till their brains squished out.

As many of the women, children, and elderly ran frantically about trying to evade the onslaught, the braves fought hard to give their tribe ample time to escape. Black Kettle was also persuaded to leave and save himself so the people that survived would have a leader to guide them. Many braves gave up their lives that day in order for others to flee to safety.

About two hundred innocent people were murdered and their bodies desecrated and mutilated in every way possible that day November 29 1864. Colonel Chivington bragged about his exploits and even stood on a stage in Devenvor, in front of a large crowd, as he displayed over one hundred scalps and also women's pubic hair. Word got back to Govorner Evans of what Chivington had done, but all the Colonel ever got was a reprimand and he was asked to resign from his position. Although Chivington never regretted what he had done to the natives, the natives were angry that he didn't get punished for his devilish deeds, but Black Kettle still desired peace with the white man and spoke against retaliation when the Cheyenne wanted to fight back.

Katelyn wondered how colonels and majors could get away scot free with murderous acts of mercilessly killing off the natives. It wasn't fair that the government only gave them a slight slap on the wrist and they never looked at it again. Since she was into reading about natives being mistreated Katelyn decided to read a couple more documents on that subject.

The winter of 1862 - 1863 was a very cold and harsh winter. With the coming of the white man the Northern Shoshone Indians were finding it hard to survive. There had not been enough buffalo for them to lay up stores for the winter. Now in January 1863 Chief Sagwitch was at his wits end about what to do. A nearby friendly residence had stopped giving them food because there were groups of natives who had stolen cattle and horses to eat. Chief

Sagwitch knew of the thefts and was highly against such dealings. Some of his own band, only a handful, had participated in the stealing, even though the Chief had strictly forbidden such misgivings. He knew that his people would die if they didn't get food soon, but he refused to take from the white man.

Brave Bear, one of the Shoshone elders, upon entering Chief Sagwitch's teepee, grunted, "There is a white man here that wants to speak to you Oh Great Chief."

Chief Sagwitch looked up from the fire into which he had been staring deep in thought," Let him come inside and we will talk."

Brave Bear opened the teepee flap and beckoned the young man to come in. He was a man in his early twenties. His sandy blond hair was tied back in a ponytail which hung down his back. His blue eyes darted from side to side as he stepped into the teepee.

Chief Sagwitch, detecting the nervousness of the young man, smiled before he spoke. "You have nothing to be afraid of my son," he spoke gently while gesturing for the young man to sit across the fire from him. "You have come to talk with me. What is your name?"

Bill Ogden Sir," Bill looked at the Chief

"Well Bill Ogden," the Chief grinned. "I know your father, and that you live very close to us, so what is it you want to talk about?"

Feeling more at ease with what the Chief had just said, Bill replied, "We just got word from Brigham City that the Cavalry is coming to Bear River."

"Are they coming to gather those who took part in stealing the white mans cattle and horses for food?" the Chief inquired.

"All I can tell you, Chief, "Bill suggested, "They are coming to punish the deeds of theft."

"Maybe the man in charge of the Cavalry will be a reasonable man," Chief Sagwitch smiled. "Thank you Bill Ogden for coming here to tell us about the Cavalry coming."

"You're welcome Sir," Bill smiled at the Chief. When my father came back from Brigham City with supplies, he told me to ride out here to tell you about the Cavalry."

"You are a brave young warrior," the Chief encouraged Bill. "You go thank your father for his concern for us."

"Many of our people are angry with the Indians for stealing our livestock." Bill explained. "But my father does not believe that it is your band that is stealing."

Chief Sagwitch had risen and come to stand beside Bill who had also risen. "It breaks my heart," the Chief placed his hand on Bill's shoulder as he spoke, "There are some of those in my band who joined the others who did the stealing. I am willing to give the Cavalry those who helped to take the white mans cattle and horses."

"Let's hope the Cavalry is happy with your decision," Bill replied.

"Bill Ogden," the Chief spoke reassuringly, "You tell your father that we are thankful for his concern over us. Go in peace my son, and may we always be your friend."

After Bill left, Chief Sagwitch called together a counsel meeting. He instructed his people to be prepared because he did not trust the Bluecoats. This leader might be different, but in his experience from childhood on, he had not seen too many Bluecoats who didn't want to see the Indian destroyed.

"Whatever happens," the Chief instructed, "Do not shoot first because this might be a reasonable leader."

Chief Sagwitch rose up early the morning of January 29, 1863. As he looked at the mountains, he noticed the steam descending down the mountain, and he knew the Cavalry had arrived. He quickly went through the camp informing the people to get ready, and reminding them not to shoot first.

The Chief was surprised when the Cavalry rode into camp that the leader didn't ask any questions. The Cavalry just commenced firing and the Shoshone were being slaughtered. Chief Bear Hunter, who was known to the soldiers, thought he might talk some sense into the Cavalry. This useless slaughter of the Indians was not necessary, but the soldiers would not listen. They took Bear Hunter and began to torture him. Since Bear Hunter didn't cry out during the torture, they ran a rifle bayonet through his head from ear to ear.

The wounded people of the camp urged Cheif Sagwitch to escape, so he finally took their advice after losing two horses in battle. Around three hundred Northern Shoshone were ruthlessly massacred that day, and Colonel Patrick E. Conor never got punished for his merciless act of murder.

Katelyn couldn't help but shake her head at how ruthless people could be. She understood that the natives had been ruthless in many of their dealings as well. They also attacked innocent white villages to seek revenge against the white man coming to the shores of this continent. Chief Pontiac from the Ottawa tribe was one chief who had led an uprising against the white man. He had attacked white villages and killed many innocent whites, to try and persuade the white man to return to the country they came from. Governor William Penn wanted peace with the natives, but there was a group of vigilantes, called the Paxton Boys, who went on a lawless rampage to take vengeance on all natives for what Pontiac had done. They went and massacred a number of Susquehannock natives who had always been friendly to the white man, right from their arrival to the shores of this land.

A steady knocking on the door irritated Governor William Penn as he sat in his study pondering the affairs that had taken place the past few days. The knocking came again and it angered the Governor why nobody was answering the door. Getting up from his plush chair, William Penn happened to look at the clock on the wall. It was already past eleven in the evening so it was no wonder nobody was going to the door to see who was there. The servants were already retired for the night. So who could be knocking frantically on his door at this late hour.

Upon opening the door, to his surprise, there were two Susquehannocks standing there, filled with fear. Penn could understand the fear these two were facing, because they were the only Susquehannocks left out of the tribe. One hundred fifty years prior to that date, there had been approximately seven thousand Susquehannoks alive. They had welcomed the whites with open arms and traded with them. Although they had enemies and fought often against other natives, they maintained their friendship with the whites. Small Pox had attacked this nation twice and dwindled their numbers down drastically. Between the wars with other tribes and the Small Pox epidemics, the Susquehannock tribe decreased to just a few hundred. From there, the tribe decreased to a couple dozen within the next two generations. Now there were just two standing outside the Governors house. A man and woman, both looking like death warmed over.

"Excuse me Sir," the man spoke fearfully as he looked at the ground, "my name is Michael and this is my wife Mary. Our people were slaughtered while we were away working in the fields of a Christian white man."

"Please, come inside," the Governor beckoned them.

Michael and Mary stepped nervously into a very spacious entrance way, and stood with heads bowed. They did not know if they were safe with the Governor, or if it had been him that had ordered the annihilation of their tribe after what Chief Pontiac of the Ottawas had done to the white villages.

Seeing their fear, William Penn spoke gently to them. "Do not be afraid," he assured them. "I mean you no harm. I am appalled at what the Paxton Boys did to the Susquehannock people."

"What can my wife and I do, now that we no longer have a tribe to go home to," Michael fought hard to keep from crying.

Mary was silent, but she kept dabbing at her face with a cloth to wipe away the tears. Upon hearing what had happened to the people of the Susquehannock tribe, she could not fathom being in a world where only her and her husband existed from a tribe that had been so large when the white man first arrived. There had of course, been those who had left the Susquehannock tribe to join other tribes when Small Pox started killing off her people, but they never contacted the Susquehannock again.

"Come into my study," the Governor was saying, "I will write a document of safety for both of you."

"How can that protect Mary and myself?" Michael protested.

"I will send word throughout the land, stating that you are not to be harmed in any way," the Governor promised. "Anyone who harms you in any way, will be hunted down and punished with death."

Michael thanked the Governor and Penn kept his word. Michael and Mary were safe, but when they died, the history of the Susquehannock died with them.

The fact that the Susquehannock were totally gone, after Michael and Mary, shook Katelyn up a bit. Tears of sadness rolled down her cheeks, as she thought about mankind hating so much as to totally wipe out another race.

As she dried her tears, Katelyn read another article that showed that there were still people from the Susquehannock tribe around. The people who had left to join up with other nations had told their story down through the ages, and the present day people still knew where they had come from.

Although the blood was mixed with other tribes, the blood from the Susquehannock was still alive today. It made Katelyn happy that there were still people out there that could trace their lineage to the Susquehannocks. She wondered how many other tribes got obliterated by the white mans hate for them. Although the natives were also to blame for attacking innocent villages of the white man, history reveals that from 1775 to 1890 thirty to forty thousand natives were massacred while in that same period fourteen thousand whites had been massacred by the natives.

Since she was into the history of massacres, and Rolland wasn't due back for another day or two, Katelyn decided to read about the Cypress Hills Massacre which took place June 1, 1873. Massacres weren't romantic, so her mind was not filled with thoughts of Rolland as she studied.

Food supplies had become increasingly scarce on the Prairies over the years, but the whiskey trade, for furs and buffalo robes, was going strong. Two groups of Assiniboine, one who's chief was Chief Manitupotis (Little Soldier), and the other Chief Inihan Kinyen, were camped in a valley alongside the Milk River in the Cypress Hills. The two camps consisted of about three hundred people. They were very poor people with only a few horses between the two groups.

A group of Crees had stolen about forty horses from a group of Wolfers who were coming back with their season's catch. When they arrived in the Cypress Hills on the Milk River they continued to search for their horses to no avail. There were two small log forts close by, one on the west bank of the Milk River was Able Farwell's Post, and one on the other bank, a short distance down, was that of Moses Solomon. The Wolfers were getting drunk at Able's Post, celebrating their catch of wolves for the season. The following morning they continued on with the festivities and Solomon joined them that morning.

Francois Laroche, one of the French Wolfers, came into Able's Post with the report that George Hammond's horse was missing.

Hammond swore in English and in French, "Them Indians close by these Posts are to blame for this."

"Now settle down George," Moses Solomon protested. "These Assiniboines are poor people and they wouldn't steal from you."

"They probably stole my horse to eat it," Hammond snorted. "Who else could have taken it?"

"Listen Hammond," Solomon continued to protect the nearby Indians. "I had trouble with these Assiniboines just recently. They accused me of dealing unfairly with them through trade.

They fired shots into my Post and threatened to kill the white man if we didn't leave."

"I rest my case, Solomon," Hammond replied drunkenly, "These Indians stole my horse in retaliation for what they thought was a raw deal."

"You don't understand George," Solomon continued to protest, "The natives have settled down again after their outrage with us. If you go out there in your drunken rage, people will die unnecessarily."

Hammond yelled in anger, "Don't try to stop us Solomon, we aim to get my horse back, and these red skins will pay for what they have done."

Able Farwell joined Solomon in trying to dissuade these drunken men from going to fight the natives, but they wouldn't listen as they took their Winchester and Henry repeating rifles and headed for the Indian camp. Unable to persuade the drunken Wolfers not to shoot the Assiniboines, Farwell waded across the Milk River in order to warn the natives to scatter. Labombarde, another French Wolfer, found Hammond's horse which had not been stolen but rather had wandered off.

By the time Hammond's horse had been found, it was too late to stop the men from attacking the natives. The liquor was clouding their judgement, and nobody knew who fired the first shot, but after that shot they all took it as the signal to start shooting. Men women and children ran from the camp trying desperately to reach the trees about fifty metres to the east of the camp. When the shooting was ended, about twenty natives had been massacred.

Chief Inhan Kinyen was among those who died in this battle. Not only was whiskey bad for the natives, but this was the second piece of history Katelyn had found where the drunken state of the minds of the whites had caused the needless death of innocent natives. The Cree's had stolen the horses, but the Assiniboine paid for that theft.

With tears falling from her eyes onto the keyboard of the computer, Katelyn was disgusted with the way the white race dominated all other races on the face of the earth. It seemed as though the white man had no feeling or respect for anyone who was not the same color they were. In fact, they didn't always care about their own kind either. The Titanic and other disasters Katelyn had studied, showed the lack of care about the lives of others. Oh how she hated being a white man at times. It shamed her to think that the race she belonged to was the most ignorant unloving race on the face of the Earth. If there was a Great Spirit, Katelyn believed that it saddened Him to see what the white race was doing to all other people.

Time passed by quickly, April ending and May beginning, showing forth it's beauty with the grass growing green and flowers all over showing forth their array of colours. Although she enjoyed being outside, Katelyn was too deep in her dream land to notice these changes in the landscape. April, May and June were filled with dreams and hopes of receiving word from Victoria. Between her history dreams, and her desire to marry Rolland, growing stronger with each passing day, Katelyn kept herself busy. They tried not to be alone too often, most of the time taking their own cars when they did meet, because they knew they couldn't trust their feelings to keep them from going too far. Rolland fought the desire to ask Katelyn too soon about marrying him, and Katelyn was baffled at what kept Rolland from asking the question. Her desire to be with him as his wife even outweighed her desire to go to Victoria, but she would be patient with Rolland. He was moving ahead rapidly in the firm he worked for, so she figured maybe he hadn't reached his potential dream just yet, so she wouldn't push him. Since Rolland supported her dream, the least she could do was to stand behind her man as he climbed the ladder of success.

CHAPTER FIVE

ONE SUNDAY AFTERNOON, TOWARDS the end of May, they were walking along the nature paths at the Helen Shuler Nature Park, also situated in the river bottom, in Indian Battle Park, north of the High Level Bridge. There had been a showing of live hawks, eagles, and owls at the centre. A good crowd of people had come to see the demonstration put on by the Birds of Prey society. Since it was a nice warm day, many people took advantage of the nature walks. Katelyn remarked about how people had lived in that area as they mined coal for a living. There were places where you could still see parts of foundations sticking out of the ground. What a life that must have been! Men coming home after a hard days work. Dirty from the black coal dust, and hungry for a decent hot meal. Most likely these men would not be in any sort of romantic mood after they returned from the coal mine each evening. The candle light dinners shared each night would only be out of necessity, not for romance. Of coarse there was the coal oil lamp they could eat by.

Katelyn dreamed of being a coal miner's daughter. Her dad would come home after his daily work, tired, hungry, and worn out. With half closed eyes, he would eat the meal, mother had slaved over and prepared for him. It had been a hard day for him sweating away in the bowels of the earth trying to make a living for his wife and children. It was a dirty, hard job that would give a man just barely enough to feed his family.

The men would come home to wives, although they had worked hard doing the household chores, yet longed for a decent romantic evening with their husband. They would find him most of the time too tired to think about romance. Oh, there were nights of love and passion alright, but seldom a time to just sit in the loving embrace of her husband's arms watching the sun as it painted the western horizon with different shades of pink and yellows. Katelyn couldn't even begin to imagine what it would have been like married to a coal miner, because she had never been married. She could only go by the feelings she felt for Rolland. You can't love someone and not have desires to be in their arms. Maybe being a coal miners wife was not that great.

She thought of having a conversation with her neighbour as they hung clothing on the line to dry. They shared the clothesline, because her neighbour had just moved next door a couple weeks before. Her husband worked the same shift in the mine as Katelyn's father did.

"How does your husband like the work he is doing?" Katelyn asked.

"He doesn't seem to mind it," Mary responded, "But I wish he could find something else to do."

"I know what you mean," Katelyn replied, "My father has been doing this for thirty-five years now, and at times I feel as though we don't seem to have a life together as a family. We move from place to place, whereever the work is."

"You're right Katelyn," Mary interjected, "Willy comes home and he is just plum tuckered out. There are nights when I desire to be held in his arms, and he'll have nothing to do with it, because he's so tired."

"I can't imagine what that would be like," Katelyn sighed. "My boyfriend, Rolland, works in the mine, but

I hope that someday he will find a different kind of job to do."

"It just isn't right that miners should be worked so hard that they are too tired for anything else," Mary was almost in tears.

"I can't complain though," Katelyn tried to sound comforting, "Although things haven't been easy for us, father does make sure that there is always plenty to eat, and warm clothes to wear."

"Willy doesn't let me down in that way either," Mary wiped back a tear that trickled down her cheek, "It's just that a women would like a few things from the finer side of life."

"It does seem to make it hard on the women folk," Katelyn replied."

"I agree," Mary responded miners shouldn't get married."

"I can't say that life has been all bad for us," Katelyn sounded apologetically, as she realized that she shouldn't be complaining.

"I don't want to sound negative, Mary replied, "I love Willy with all my heart, but sometimes I just desire to be held in his arms and do nothing else but to sit and enjoy the evening watching the sun go down. It would be nice to sit on the front porch beside Willy, drinking coffee quietly, as the shadows of darkness creep over us. His loving arm would be such a comfort as we enjoyed each other's company even if not a word was spoken between us."

"It's a hard life Mary," Katelyn looked at her and smiled, "But at least the men still provide for us."

"I'm sorry for sounding so ungrateful," Mary hung her head in shame.

Katelyn put down the shirt she was about to hang on the line. She understood why Mary felt the way she did, so she wrapped her arms around Mary to comfort her. Mary was heavy with child, and at times when she desired to be held by her husband, it would be hard for her to understand why he just wanted to go to bed and get some sleep. Being the oldest child out of four, Katelyn had seen her mother go through the same thing when she was pregnant with the youngest one. Katelyn couldn't remember to much about the other two pregnancies. Life as a coal miners family was not easy, but neither was that of the coal miner himself. It seemed as though you never got ahead in life doing this kind of work, and yet, they always had food to eat and clothes to wear.

Her family had lived in the Crows Nest Pass before coming to Lethbridge. Mining there was much more difficult since the coal seams ran in a slant upwards. After slaving away for a couple months in the Bellevue mine her father had decided to move to Lethbridge where even though the work was just as hard, at least the mines were running level.

Katelyn was glad at that moment to be who she was, and sharing her life with the man that she loved. Although she wasn't married to Rolland, she couldn't imagine living a life where you just dreamt of the day that your husband would have romantic feelings toward you. She and Rolland had real deep feelings for each other, but as a miner, he might be to tired at nights for romance. Of course, she didn't really know what it was like to be a coal miner's wife or daughter. She could only go by what she read in the history books, and then dream her own story of how it might have been.

Looking up at Rolland, who was facing forward as they walked, Katelyn had to smile. She smiled because of the thoughts she just had about being his wife as a coal miner, and because he was happy just walking by her side as she dreamed on. Rolland sensed that Katelyn was looking his way, so he turned to look at her. As he faced her, she quickly turned to look forward, but it was to late, because Rolland had seen the smile.

"What are you smiling about Sweetie?" he asked her.

"I was just in my own little world about one hundred years back," she replied.

"I gathered that much," Rolland laughed, "But what was it that made you suddenly look at me and smile."

"You would only laugh at me if I told you."

"Come now Sweetie, would I laugh at you?" he teased her.

"It was just a dumb thought that I had," Katelyn insisted.

"I don't believe that it was dumb if you were thinking about the past." Rolland assured her.

They had stopped at the rivers edge, and Rolland took her into his arms as they faced each other. Hugging her tight, he could feel her heart throbbing against his chest. If only this moment could last forever, and time could stop for eternity as they were locked together in a loving embrace. Their eyes met, and slowly their faces came together. As their lips touched, flames of passion leaped in his body with a burning desire to consume Katelyn.

Every fibre in Rollands body cried out for the ultimate, while his mind fought hard to gain control. He could tell on Katelyn's unwillingness to let go of him that she too was almost at the brink of no return. In a final and last attempt to gain control, his mind cried out, 'Get a grip of yourself!'

Katelyn's chest heaved with rythmaic waves of yielding desire. Every inch of flesh on her body, tingling with anticipation, was screaming at her to let herself go. All the times she had imagined Rolland being her lover as a brave, or a coal miner, now erupted within her, and there seemed to be no return as each minute intensified that final moment of rapturous bliss awaiting them. Why couldn't he just propose to her. Her mind was tormented with desire to be his wife.

Although that feeling had engulfed them before, it had always been easy, till today, not to get too closely involved. It was as though all time had stopped and that Katelyn and Rolland were the only two people left on the earth. The moment of rapturous bliss was upon them and neither one of them was in control anymore as Katelyn was willing to give her body over to Rolland. She was tearing at Rollands shirt when suddenly, with alarm bells frantically going off in his head Rolland, gasping for breath, pushed her away.

"I'm sorry Sweetie," Rolland managed to speak, between gasps of air, as he tried hard to get control on his throbbing heart. "I never intended to let my passion for you get me to lose control of my senses."

Her lungs burned as she fought to control her own breathing. "Honey, it's okay," Katelyn squeezed his hand. "Nothing happened, and it was not just your doing."

"But I should have had better control of my emotions," Rolland insisted. "I know the strong commitment we made together, and I want to fulfill that commitment."

Katelyn laughed joyously as she looked directly into Rollands eyes. "Look here you big hunk of compassionate love, do you think that I didn't desire to have you today, or any day, as a matter of fact? Now stop blaming yourself. We didn't do anything wrong, and besides, I shouldn't have led you on."

"You are such a wonderfully beautiful young lady, Katelyn. I don't know what I would do without you." Rolland took her hand and kissed it.

Katelyn was thinking about his remark and smiled as the words formed in her mind, 'Propose to me you romantic fool, and I promise you that you'll never be without me.' All Roland would have to do was ask the question, and Katelyn would give him a definite, 'Yes.' What was he waiting for anyway?

Taking preventive measures not to fall into deeper temptation, they left Indian Battle Park. On the way to Kaitlyn's car, neither one of them spoke a word as they both were lost in their own thoughts about how wonderful it had been to be together in near rapturous bliss that evening.

Katelyn sighed as she thought back again at the scene of Jack and Rose in the back of that old car. She could imagine Rose's lungs nearly bursting, her breast pressed firmly against his naked chest, while her heart throbbed at that final moment of rapturous bliss.

Rolland, hearing her deep sigh, didn't dare look at Katelyn for fear his heart would come apart, as the deep desire to consume her with all he had, burned deep within his whole being at that moment. If he looked at her, he might not be able to control his emotions. If only she would receive word from Victoria that she had the job, then he could be assured that that part of her dream was done.

When they got to her car, they didn't embrace each other or kiss goodnight. They both knew, without saying a word, that it was for the best that they parted quickly. Katelyn waited till Rolland drove away before she stepped into her car. Her heart was still racing as she drove home. What a night this had been for the both of them. Even after she had turned in for the night, Katelyn's heart soared as she lay in her bed not being able to sleep. She pondered over what might have been had Rolland not pushed her away before it was to late. At that moment, nothing had mattered to her, as her body had been prepared to go all the way. Her organs had screamed out of anguish not to stop, but then in one breath that moment of ecstasy had been swept away as Rolland had shoved her away from him. For one brief moment she became angry as she thought maybe Rolland didn't desire her body, but then she reminded herself of how Rolland had kissed her and was in the process of starting to caress her body ever so gently before he suddenly pushed away from her. How could she ever think that Rolland didn't desire her? He respected her desire to wait till marriage. So what was he waiting for?

Sighing with relief that it had ended when it did, she still felt a pang of pain as she thought about the abrupt stop. She wondered what it would have been like engulfed in a rapturous eruption of love and desire for each other, but Katelyn knew it was better this way. What if Rolland never intended on marrying her? Although the experience could have been total ecstasy for the moment, it would leave lasting scars forever, because Katleyn would always be reminded of how she had allowed her body to be shared with someone else than her husband. The thought of Rolland not marrying her, left Katelyn in a cold and terrifying sweat. She shuddered at the thought. "You fool," she breathed out in a whisper, "Why don't you ask me to marry you?"

"Stop thinking like that," Katelyn scolded herself speaking into the darkness. "After all, he gave you that locket. Doesn't that account for his desire to be with you! He's just not ready to pop the question yet."

With that said, Katelyn closed her eyes to try and sleep. She had a restless night as her mind was plagued with dreams of Rolland taking her in his arms. As they became lost in each others embrace, her dreams were shattered as each time Rolland pushed her away. Katelyn's body was perspiring as she woke up to realize it was only a dream. She would lay awake for a few moments getting control of her feelings before drifting off to sleep again. As the night wore on, and the dreams kept waking her up, Katelyn was beginning to become very upset over these dreams and what they meant. Why did she have to dream the same thing over so many times. It had been bad enough to dream it once, so was this then an omen of what was to come? The natives believed strongly in dreams and visions. Did this mean she would never experience the ecstasy of sexual bliss with Rolland? Was she only going to have thoughts of what might have been? The experience of the evening before, plus the dreams during the night, left Katelyn in a foul mood.

Getting out of bed, Katelyn went straight into the shower. She hoped that she would feel better after the refreshing water washed her body from all that perspiration.

Katelyn stood there a few minutes letting the water engulf her body while she reflected on the dreams she had. Her mind was still tormenting her with thoughts of Rolland never proposing to her. It made her angry to think that she had almost lost her virginity to a man who might never have intentions of marrying her. She knew it was foolish to think this way, but her restless night didn't help in making her happy. By the time her shower was over, she was furious with herself for not having better control over her emotions, but it was hard to hold back when you were so in love with someone. Why didn't he just propose to her? That was the question that forever haunted her, and it didn't help Katelyn's emotions at that moment either.

The ringing of the phone startled her. It was Rolland. Katelyn almost snapped at him, but caught herself just in time before tearing a strip off of him. Although this was not a good time for Rolland to be talking to her, she needed to stay in control of her feelings. If she lost it now, Katelyn might also lose Rolland. It wasn't his fault she had these dreams. Or was it?

"Sweetie," Rolland spoke calmly, "Are you alright?"

"I'll be fine," Katelyn snapped back.

"You sound a bit upset."

"I'll be alright," Katelyn insisted sternly.

"Was it something I did?" Rolland questioned.

"Yes and no," Katelyn tried hard to control herself.

Katelyn didn't want to be hard on Rolland, but the dreams had an impact on her mood. She knew she would have to collect her thoughts and let Rolland know that she was alright. It wasn't fair to treat him this way because of some dreams.

"Sweetie," Rolland broke into her thoughts, "Shall I pick you up for lunch so we can discuss this."

Although her mood was not one of the best, it was still good to hear Rolland's voice. Katelyn was angry with herself for letting her thoughts dictate her feelings to her. "I'll be waiting for you," she replied as cheerful as she could.

Rolland hung up the phone almost hesitant to do so. Katelyn had never sounded this way to him before. Was she angry with him for stopping them before they went too far last night? He couldn't fathom her being angry over that, because she had insisted that she would only be intimate with her husband. What was bothering Katelyn, puzzled him. Her behaviour made it hard for him to concentrate on his work as he pondered over what it might be that had her in a snit.

Katelyn had put down the phone after Rolland hung up. She lay across her bed and thought about how she must have sounded to Rolland. It bothered her, because she didn't want to lose him. He meant the world to her, and he was so understanding. She had dated other guys, but all they wanted from her was her body. They didn't care about her, because as soon as she had refused them the use of her body, they would dump her. Rolland wasn't that way, so why was she angry with him. He was so understanding of how she felt and what she wanted out of life. Yet it left her bewildered, why couldn't he just ask her to marry him?

Suddenly, she burst into tears. She thought of calling him back and apologizing for the way she had sounded, but at that moment she was too emotional to even talk to him. Here she was blaming Rolland for her dreams. It wasn't his fault that her dreams turned out the way they did. He respected her desire to refrain from being intimate until marriage, and last night he honoured that desire by stopping when he did, and by leaving her by her car instead of pursuing a lengthy goodnight kiss.

Katelyn sobbed herself to sleep. She slept so soundly, that she didn't even hear the knock on her door. Again the knock came, and still she slept on. She was dreaming of riding a fluffy cloud through the sky. All anger and malice were gone from her. There wasn't a care in the world that could arouse her now, but then, she wasn't in the world.

She was far above the world in a sky filled with cotton like clouds with nobody to disturb her. The thought all at once dawned on her, 'Where was everybody else.' In fact, there was not even a sound to be heard in this fluffy world of hers, but wait, was that the sound of a telephone faintly ringing. Looking around from cloud to cloud for the phone, Katelyn couldn't see one, and yet the ringing didn't quit. Why couldn't she find the phone?

Realization that the phone in her room was really ringing, Katelyn bolted upright as she rolled over in her bed. She was still laying crosswise on her stomach, so it took a moment for her to get herself together enough to grab the phone. Fumbling with her hand on the night stand, her head still in a daze, Katelyn got a hold of the phone.

"Hello," she managed to say sleepily."

"Sweetie," Rollands voice came to her through the fog in her head. "Are you alright?"

"Ya--ya, I----I'm fine," Katelyn managed to say as she tried to gather her thoughts.

"I knocked on your door," Rolland replied, "But you didn't answer so I'm calling you on my cell."

"I'm sorry Honey," Katelyn was fully awake now. "I guess I dozed off after talking to you earlier."

Getting up, Katelyn opened the door for Rolland, but asked him to wait outside while she freshened up a bit. She had never let any boy into her apartment and Rolland knew that, so he waited patiently outside for her. Katelyn quickly splashed water on her face, straightened up her hair, and then picking up her purse, she followed Rolland to the car. As they drove to the restaurant, Katelyn explained the dreams to Rolland and told him that she had been angry from having a restless night. She assured him that she was sorry for sounding angry with him, but Rolland just teased her and laughed it off. He reminded Katelyn that he respected her feelings, and that he would do everything in his power to never let anything happen to hurt those feelings. He informed her that she probably dreamt those dreams because neither one of them wanted to hurt the other.

Katelyn couldn't help admiring Rolland for the way he treated her. How could she ever doubt his love for her. It still puzzled her why he didn't propose to her, but she wouldn't pressure him into it. She realized that Rolland had to sort out his own thoughts about marriage. When he felt ready for it, he surly would sweep her off her feet by asking her the big question that all girls desired to hear.

As they ate lunch, Rolland informed Katelyn that he had to leave town again for a few days. He would be leaving in the morning as the company was flying him to Victoria to see a new client who was interested in the Firm for his business accounting. Although Katelyn hated to see him go, she realized that a few days apart would be good for both of them. It wasn't like he would be gone forever. She would just let herself get lost in some era where she would be too busy to think about Rolland. Of course that would be almost next to impossible seeing as most of her historical fantasies involved Rolland.

After lunch, Rolland headed back to work, and Katelyn decided to go to the museum and volunteer her time there till she had to go to work. The hours passed by quickly, and her imagination kept her so intrigued that she felt sad that it was almost time to go to work. Just before she left, she stopped at the museum souvenir shop to buy two books that she believed would be of interest to her. One of them was, "Boats & Barges on the Belly," put out by the Lethbridge Historical Society, and the other book was, "LETHBRIDGE Its Coal Industry," written by Alex Johnston, Keith G. Gladwyn, and L. Gregory Ellis.

Her shift went by quickly, and after getting home, she read for a little while about the coal industry in

Lethbridge, and also about the boats and barges that carried the coal from Lethbridge to Medicine Hat until the a small gauge railway was built in 1885. The coal was then taken by rail from Lethbridge to Dunmore which was a short distance from Medicine Hat.

The following morning proved to be a beautiful day, so Katelyn packed a lunch and drove down to Indian Battle Park, where she took out her two newly purchased books, and buried her nose into the history behind coal mining and transporting coal on the river to Medicine Hat. It wasn't long before she was once again dreaming about being a coal miners daughter.

CHAPTER SIX

THERE NEVER SEEMED TO be a lack of washing to do, as the miners came home everyday from work covered in coal dust. The women folk sure had their share of cleaning to do, as well as getting breakfast ready, making lunches for the men, and preparing the evening meal, plus watching the children. The men slaved away at making a living so that the family was fed, clothed, and educated, but there never seemed to be much extra money left over. Katelyn was taking clothes off the line, while dreaming about the life she desired to have with Rolland. That was of course, if he ever asked her to marry him. She hated the thought of Rolland working in a mine all his life. Although her father had provided well for them, she desired to marry a man who was capable of doing more than work in a mine to support a family. She didn't blame her father for not knowing anything other than mining, because her grandfather had also been a miner. Papa didn't have much education, because his father had made him work the mines at a very early age. According to Papa, those had been hard times and he had to work to help support their family. Papa had been the oldest of seven children, and her grandpa needed Papa's help to bring in enough money for survival. Even then it had been just enough to make ends meet. Papa had talked often about his growing up and had promised that his children would not have to quit school to help the financial need of his family. It was hard sometimes, but Papa had always provided the necessities of life.

Rolland was trying to get ahead by doing some night classes that were being provided. A local teacher, Mr. Hamalton, was willing to devote his time and effort into teaching those who wanted to further their education. Since Rolland desired to study, he had applied to take the course, and he had been eccepted. There was a small fee to be paid for taking the evening classes, so many men who would have liked to take it couldn't. Rolland on the other hand, didn't care what it cost him. He wanted to move ahead in life. He would soon have the education needed to continue on with an accounting course, which he also planned to take time to do in the evenings with

Mr. Hamalton's help. Katelyn believed that Rolland could make it far in life as something besides a miner.

After Katelyn had taken off the last piece of clothing from the line, she bent down to pick up the basket, when suddenly, a shadow of a man appeared on the ground from behind her. Startled by the sudden appearance of the shadow, Katelyn stood up quickly, and whirling around, she faced the man behind her. To her surprise, it was Rolland.

"You startled me," Katelyn gasped.

"I'm sorry Sweetie," Rolland spoke reassuringly

"Why aren't you at work today?" Katelyn couldn't help wonder what might have kept Rolland off the job.

"Last night, before going home, I took a walk beside the river, and I noticed two new steamers moored to the dock," Rolland was as excited as a little boy at Christmas time.

"So what's so exciting about two new steamers to keep you from work," Katelyn inquired.

"This morning I took the chance of staying home from the mine, and checking to see if there was any work available on one of the steamers," Rolland grinned as he spoke.

"From the grin on your face," Katelyn interrupted him, "You got a job on the steamer."

"That's right," Rolland grabbed Katelyn and spun her around, catching her in his powerful arms. "Captain Wesley Todd gave me a job aboard the Steamer Alberta."

"What about your classes?" Katelyn was concerned that Rolland would be unable to finish his night courses working on the steamer. They would be gone at least a couple days or more.

"I spoke with Mr. Hamalton about it," Rolland replied gleefully. "He assured me that he would be willing to spend time with me to finish the course at my leisure because he likes "My zest for learning," as he put it.

"Oh Rolland," Katelyn placed a loving kiss on his cheek, "I'm so glad that you are no longer going underground to make a living."

"Mining isn't such a bad job," Rolland laughed at Katelyn's concern for him. "Although I would rather be on top of the ground than underneath it."

"It might not be a bad job," Katelyn playfully scolded him, "but people die in the coal mines."

"People die on river boats too," Rolland teased.

"Now you stop talking like that," Katelyn scolded as she looked him straight in the eye. "I won't be able to sleep a wink knowing that you might be in danger on that steamer."

"Katelyn Sweetie," Rolland hugged her tightly in his arms, "Nothing will happen to me out there on the water."

"So when do you leave for Medicine Hat?" Katelyn questioned.

"They're loading the steamers now, and once they have the load capacity they can carry, we'll be off," Rolland smiled as Katelyn still had that concerned look on her face, "Then we will set sail for the great wild yonder, with all it's adventures to behold."

Katelyns mind was racing. She was happy about the news Rolland brought her, but yet she was concerned. It wasn't only for his life that she was concerned, just that she wouldn't see him for a few days. Although Katelyn didn't see Rolland all the time, while he worked in the mine, he was close enough to her that if she wanted to see him, she could go to his home. Out on the steamer it would be different, because he would be gone away from Coalbanks for a while. That thought brought tears to her eyes. She was happy that at that very moment she was in Rollands arms, because that way he couldn't see the tears. When he let go of her, she quickly bent down to pick up the empty clothes basket but Rolland stopped her. As she came back up, Rolland noticed the tear streaked face and took it for granted that they were tears of joy over his new job.

"Everything will be alright sweetie," he teased her. "The job will only last two or three months because they can only use the river when the water is high. In July the run off from the mountains will be less so the steamers won't be able to operate on the river again till the next year."

Katelyn sighed as she brushed away the tears and dried her face with the apron she wore. "I'm just so happy that you won't be in the mine anymore."

"Oh, after the steamers quit using the river, I might have to work the mine again till I complete my accounting course," Rolland laughed.

Rolland picked up the clothes basket and carried it to the house for Katelyn. Together they shared with her mother the good news about Rollands new job. Katelyn's mother was happy for him. She had so desired that her own husband would have been able to do something else besides coal mining. He had mined out East, and when word had come about miners needed at Bellevue, they had moved. They had hoped that the new area would also bring with it a new life.

When they heard about miners needed in the Coalbanks area, they moved again because the mine at Bellevue was hard to work in. The coal seams ran along at a slant because it was in a mountain. Since Coalbanks was on the Prairie, the seams were level and much easier to work. The coal here was softer as well, so it was less work to break it lose.

Katelyn's mother sighed as she said out loud, "Coal Towns will always be Coal Towns."

"What was that," Katelyn asked in surprise to her mothers comment.

"Oh Honey, I was just thinking of how nice it could have been if your father was something other than a coal miner," her mother replied.

"Why did you ever marry dad, if you hate coal mining so much?" Katelyn asked her mother.

"Well Honey, it's this way," her mother began, "When you are in love with someone, you really don't care what sort of work they do. Your father was a coal miner when I first met him, and although I knew very little about mining, I did know that it was dirty hard work. Your father was a real romancer, and I just loved the way he treated me. Over the years I got used to his line of work, but that doesn't mean I don't sometimes long for a different kind of life."

"It is amazing that you could last this long with someone if you hate coal mining so much," Katelyn insisted.

"Honey," mother smiled lovingly at her daughter, "When you love someone the way I love your father, nothing can separate the two of you. You might long for a better life, but that doesn't change the love you have for the man that works hard to provide for his family. He has never stopped treating me with love and respect."

"I have seen that love flow out of you," Katelyn gave her mother a big hug of appreciation "I love you mom," she whispered

"I love you too, Honey," mother replied.

When the Steamer 'Alberta' was loaded down with coal, Katelyn accompanied Rolland to the dock to see him off. Rolland introduced her to Captain Wesly Todd, and to the other crew members. One of the crew was an Irishman named Ira McDougle, who seemed to be in his glory when he could tease someone. As she kissed Rolland to send him on his way, the Irishman laughed heartily as he spoke to Katelyn.

"We'll take good care of your lad, Miss.," he laughed as Rolland boarded the Steamer. "Nothing will happen to him. In fact, we will work him so hard that he won't even notice the pretty girls around."

"I have nothing to fear where other girls are concerned," Katelyn replied.

"Ah, but Miss.," Ira teased, "He'll be away from you for a few days."

"Absence makes the heart grow fonder," Katelyn responded.

"Well Miss., I can't argue with you on that point," Ira chuckled, "But just in case we spot a beautiful native lass along the way, I'll try to hold your lad down." Ira burst out laughing at the expression on Katelyn's face, then he added, "Just in case he has ideas of jumping overboard."

"Just you make sure that no harm comes to my so called lad," Katelyn pointed a playful finger at Ira, "Or else you'll have me to deal with."

Turning to Rolland, Ira winked at him and said, "It looks as though you have a feisty lass on your hands mate."

"Ira," Rolland played along with the tease, "She could probably take you on, no problem at all."

Everybody laughed and then Captain Todd gave the word to shove off, at which time Katelyn left the deck of the steamer. The ropes were hauled on board, after which the engine throbbed ever so gently below deck, and the paddle wheel began to churn the waters. The steamer moved slowly away from the dock, and when it cleared safely, Captain Todd gave the word, "Full speed ahead."

Katelyn watched as the Steamer moved down the river, and before it went around the bend, she gave her final wave to Rolland who stood watching her. He returned the wave, and then as he blew her a kiss, the steamer was gone from sight. Only the engine and the churning of the paddle wheel could be heard as the Alberta moved onward towards her destination. It saddened Katelyn to know that Rolland was gone, but at the same time, she was glad that he was no longer working in the mine.

When she arrived back home, Katelyn changed into her working cloths. She had put on a pretty dress to see Rolland off, and now that he was gone, she had her household chores to help with. Katelyn knew that if she kept herself busy, the time would go by faster. Although Rolland had been gone less than an hour, she already missed him. She desired so much to hear him ask her to marry him.

Rolland's life on the steamer was short lived, like Rolland had said it would be. The Alberta was only able to make eight trips to Medicine Hat before the water in the river was too low for travel. Although the Alberta and other steamers were used to transport troops and supplies on other rivers and lakes, Rolland ended his steamer career after the last trip from Coal Banks to Medicine Hat. Captain Wesly Todd had all but begged Rolland to stay on with them, but Rolland knew that would mean being away from Katelyn for a couple months, not days. It was also his concern to get his bookkeeping course completed. Staying with the crew on the Alberta could mean forfeiting his degree in accounting. He decided that it would be better to work the mines for a short period until he completed the course.

Working on the steamer had been a good experience for Rolland. There were times that the Alberta would run aground on a sand bar. At these times, it took much hard work to set her free again. There were men on either side of the steamer, as well as in the front, that would take constant soundings of the depth of the water. Men were constantly singing out six feet, four feet, one foot, etc., thus enabling the Captain to manoeuver the steamer through the water. Although soundings were being taken carefully, there were still times the sand bars would come up as a surprise.

Although he didn't want to return to the mines, Rolland knew that he had to work at something in order to make a living. He also hoped that after completing the course, there would be an opening in that field of work for him. Sir Alexander Galt had caught wind of this young man's ambition of becoming a bookkeeper. He was well aware of the fact that Rolland would study hard after each return trip on the Alberta. When he had successfully completed the training needed to be a successful accountant, Sir Alexander Galt gave Rolland the job of being his own personal bookkeeper. Rolland was in his glory. All the hard work and studying was finally going to pay off.

After Rolland started working for Sir Alexander Galt, Katelyn believed strongly in her heart that he would propose to her. After all, he was making very good money now, so nothing should stand in the way of them being married. What a joy that would be, to be able to spend the rest of her life with the man who she really deeply loved and admired. Surely now he would place that ring upon her finger.

Katelyn came out of her dream world as she closed the history books on mining and steamers. What an awesome dream it had been. She was glad that times had changed, and that although people still had to work, they could still take time out to enjoy life. The thought suddenly hit her, maybe people were more at peace back one hundred years ago than they were in this day and age. Back then they worked hard at life, where as these days people seemed to have more leisure time on their hands. Not that she was complaining about how things were today, just that there seemed to be a greater closeness or bonding together back then. These days everybody seemed to be out only for themselves.

Putting her books aside, Katelyn took her bag lunch and began to eat. It had been an interesting time at the park, reliving by-gone days when coal was being extracted from the bowels of the earth in Southern Alberta. As she bit into her sandwich, Katelyn thought about the mine disasters that claimed the lives of many miners over a period of time. She would have to stop over at the library, before work, to find some books on the subject of mine disasters.

As she left Indian Battle Park, the thought came to her about going to the Crows Nest Pass to visit the Frank Slide Interpretive centre the following day, since it was Saturday and she was off for the weekend. With that decided, she checked the library for some books and took a couple with her.

The thought of going to visit Frank Slide was heavy on her mind, so she couldn't get into the books she had taken home from the library. This would be a good night to go to bed early, since Frank Slide was one and a half hours west of Lethbridge.

Katelyn lay awake till the clock showed nearly two in the morning. She tried to convince herself to sleep, but her mind was a constant buzz about her trip to the Crows Nest Pass. The more she thought about the trip, the more she was convinced that she should also stop at Hillcrest, to visit the town where the worst mine disaster in Canada had happened. Hillcrest was only a couple minutes drive from the town of Frank. This was going to be an adventurous day for Katelyn.

She finally fell asleep and managed to get about five hours as she had set her alarm at seven AM. That way she had time to shower, eat, and get ready to be on the road by eight thirty. That would give her just enough time to arrive at the interpretive centre when the doors opened at ten.

Her trip proved to be more interesting than she had imagined. At Frank Slide she learned that one side of Turtle Mountain had slid down covering a vast area of the town of Frank. After the mountain side slid down, they estimated that seventy-six people were killed but only twelve bodies were recovered. It all happened April 29, 1903. They believed that mining within the bowels of the mountain caused the slide to happen. The slide would have happened even if mining hadn't sped it along, because the Natives had called the mountain Turtle Mountain saying that it was the Mountain that moves. Even the Natives wouldn't pitch their teepee's under this mountain. The white man with all his smart ways had built the town of Frank under it, and when a part of the mountain broke off, in just over one and a half minutes the town was buried. Seventeen miners were trapped inside the mountain for thirteen hours before they finally dug their way out of the side of the mountain that moves.

Hillcrest, which had experienced the worst mine disaster in the history of Canada, proved to be well worth the stop over as Katelyn took time to visit the area where all the bodies were buried together in one large grave. On June 19, 1914, an explosion in the mine took the lives of one hundred eighty-nine miners. This disaster left one hundred thirty women as widows, and four hundred children fatherless.

Driving away from Hillcrest, Katelyn drove by Bellevue and remembered something about a mine tour in that town. Bellevue was another old coal town that was only moments away from Hillcrest and Frank Slide. Although it was very cold in the mine where the tour took place, Katelyn experienced first hand what it was like to be underground with just a small lamp on the helmet they provided. As the guide took them deeper and deeper under ground, he explained everything that took place in the mine when it was operational. When the bottom fell out of the coal industry, they just left everything in the mine and closed it up. The part of the mine that they used for touring, was well shored up with timbers, and at the end there was a wire mesh fence preventing the tourist from going further. The guide explained that further down the tunnel, had water in it, but also that the coal cars had just been left there to rust and rot away in the water. The tourists were asked to turn off their lamps, and upon doing so the tunnel was left in total darkness. It gave Katelyn an eerie feeling even though there were others standing in the darkness with her. This was not a place she wanted to let her imagination go into dream mode.

As Katelyn drove home after her day of adventure, she was happy that she had taken time to check out these sites. There were other things of interest she could have spent time at,but she wanted to get home before it got too late. Maybe she could spend some time travelling around the internet to check on other mine disasters in the world.

When Rolland came home, he was kept very busy on setting up the new client account he had just acquired in Victoria. His boss was so happy with the success of obtaining this companies business, because the owners were tough to deal with, that he gave Rolland a hefty raise. After getting the account set up in the computers, Rolland had to take another trip to Victoria to go over all the books with the CEO of the company. This could take a week, he told Katelyn, but she assured him she would be alright, even though she would miss him while he was gone. They had not spent too much time in Indian Battle Park alone since the last episode there. Whenever they did go, it would be during peak times when others were there with their children.

Katelyn decided that she would find some history that was not romantically inclined. Then she could bury her nose in it and not be tempted to involve Rolland. With Rolland gone, she could hide in her dream world and make the time pass by quicker until his return.

Rolland had to catch his flight early Wednesday morning, but Katelyn had insisted to be there to see him off. As they held each other tightly, Katelyn's body quivered with fresh excitement. Oh how she desired to be intimate with this man.

As she released her hold on Rolland, she whispered, "Sorry my love. If I don't let you go now, I promise you that you will miss your flight."

Rolland, speechless for a moment, smiled at her. When he finally got back his composure, he laughed, but only to hide his own deep desires of the moment. Clearing his throat, he whispered back to her, "I understand Sweetie. Your touch is electrifying. It draws upon every fibre of my being desiring to lose myself in eternal bliss as we frolic together in never ending love."

"I will miss you my love," Katelyn spoke as she tried to calm her emotions.

Choked with desire to unleash his love upon the girl he cherished, Rolland smiled as he replied, "I will miss you more." With that, he moved on towards the departure gate. Looking back once before going through security he saw, Katelyn still standing watching him, so he blew her a kiss and then he moved on.

CHAPTER SEVEN

KATELYN WENT TO HUMPTYS, for breakfast, on the south side of the city, since it was on the way back from the airport. She very seldom had breakfast in a restaurant, except when away on vacation. Since she was up early to see Rolland off on his flight, she decided that a treat was in order. As she ate breakfast, Kately pondered over different areas of history that she could study, that would not get Rolland romantically involved. As she searched the deep recesses of her memory, Katelyn could not come up with one idea that would help her find something in history that could keep her mind off Rolland. As she was about to give up on the idea her eye caught a painting on the wall in front of her. In the painting, she saw a tall ship fighting fiercely against the wave of a storm. Katelyn counted three large masts on her, but the sails were down to wait out the storm. She wondered what it would be like to battle fierce winds and waves on a tall ship. The waves were threatening to capsize the ship, but in the painting you could see she was putting up a good fight. Although the idea of tall ships was a good subject to study, Katelyn quickly put that thought out of her mind. She knew that before long she would have Rolland being the Captain of a tall ship while she waited day in and day out for his safe return. She could not bear to see the man, she loved and cherished, fighting fierce waves as the ship in the painting was doing. Katelyn shuddered as she thought of Rolland sinking with his ship because she had heard often that the captain goes down with the ship.

The waitress, who was pouring Katelyn another cup of coffee, seeing her shudder, questioned Katelyn, "Are you alright, Miss."

Katelyn, blushing at her sudden reaction to her thoughts, replied, "Yes, thank you. I just had a strange thought cross my mind."

"Is there anything else I can get for you today?" the waitress asked.

"No thank you," Katelyn replied politly. "I should be good for now."

Having a vivid imagination can sure be embarrassing sometimes, she thought as she continued to finish her breakfast. The thought suddenly came to her from out of nowhere. She could study pirates. Pirates sailed tall ships, but she could never imagine a pirate being romantic, and there was definitely no way she could imagine Rolland as one of these fierce men. These were death defying men who plundered other ships, raping women and slitting their throats afterwards. There were also brothels where these pirates could go to relieve their sexual desires with women who had no romantic feelings towards them. There was no romance in the deeds, and acts of piracy, only barbaric acts of self indulgence. Rolland could never be such a man. He was just to good for her to see him in such acts of indecency. After all, pirates were rough and tough men who couldn't be romantic. How could she ever picture Rolland as a pirate? That seemed almost next to impossible to imagine. Katelyn laughed out loud at the thought of Rolland out on the ocean plundering ships for their goods. She was aware that people were looking at her after her outburst of laughter, but she didn't care. She was a young lady with a wild, free and adventurous imagination. She could travel places without even leaving the city.

The waitress never questioned Katelyn about her sudden outburst of laughter. She figured it was none of her business how people felt or thought. Handing Katelyn the bill, she just carried on with her work.

Katelyn paid for her breakfast and decided to go to the library to search for books on pirates. The library opened at 9:00 a.m., and it was nearly 8:45 now. By the time she drove down town, she would be in time for the doors to open.

As Katelyn entered the library, she headed straight for the computers to find as many books as she could on pirates. The ladies at the information desk greeted her as she went by, and Katelyn just smiled in response. She was well known in the library, because of the frequent visits she made there. Finding some good titles, Katelyn gathered together three books that would help her discover the life styles of those Buccaneers that roved the sea for plunder. She sat in the library for about five hours reading and dreaming about the adventure of a pirate. Having an hour to spare before she had to be at work, Katelyn took the books and went to Humptys downtown for a quick bite to eat. In her excitement about pirates, she had forgotten to stop for lunch. It had been no wonder, not only had her imagination run wild, she learned things she never imagined possible.

To her surprise, Katelyn found the names of two women who had become pirates. Finding this to be of interest, Katelyn started to read about the life and exploits of Anne Bonney, and Mary Read. Anne was the offspring of an Irish attorney, William Cormac, and a household maid Peg Brennan. After getting the maid pregnant and losing a great deal of respect from all his clients, Cormac took the maid and moved to America where he settled in Carolina. He followed his profession for a while and then became a merchant where he made enough money to buy a large plantation. After the death of the maid; Anne's mother; Anne, who was about thirteen or fourteen at the time helped to look after the affairs of her father.

Anne was a beautiful redhead who attracted many rich young boys, as well as the poor ones, to come and ask for her hand in marriage. Being a spitfire didn't stop the boys from coming around. On one occasion a young boy filled with passion and desire for the tempestuous redhead, tried to rape her. To his surprise, Anne turned the tables on him and assaulted him with such furry that he was bedridden for weeks afterward. Anne was after what she wanted, not what others wanted for her.

Anne married James Bonney, a young sailor, against her fathers wishes. Her inheritance from her father was a very substantial amount, but because she married that poor sailor who had nothing but the clothes on his back, her father disowned her and put her out of his house. Since she was no longer welcome in her father's house, Anne and her husband boarded a ship and headed for the island of Providence. Anne soon grew tired of her life with her husband. She wanted to have some adventure out at sea. She began to hang out with the pirates that rendezvoused at Nassau a port of Providence.

One day, Captian Rackam, a notorious pirate, came to Nassau to receive the king's pardon that had been promised to any pirate who would serve in helping to fight against the Spanish invasion. Woodes Rogers, who was the Governor at that time, refused to give pardon to Captian Racham because he was not sure if he could trust this pirate. Racham, believing that he would receive his pardon in due time, went about drinking in the waterfront taverns with old friends. It was here that his eyes fell on Anne Bonney, and instantly he desired to have her for himself.

Calico Jack, as Captain Jack Racham was nickname because of the colourful clothing he always wore, was also a very attractive man, and it didn't take Anne long to fall in love with him. Racham offered to pay James Bonney for his wife, but Bonney refused the offer. Bonney complained to Governor Rogers about Rackam seducing his young wife so Calico Jack took Anne out to sea with him. Rogers had refused pardon to Rackam, so there was nothing left for him but to plunder ships at sea.

Anne, who was dressed up like a young man, stood with Captian Rackam and his men as they pillaged every ship they came in contact with. Living this reckless life intrigued Anne as she fought with fierceness, pistol in one hand and blade in the other. Although she was dressed like a man, Rackam's men knew that she was the Captian's women. They all feared what might come to them if they even touched her. Anne herself managed quite well with pistol and blade. The men saw how she fought, and no one dared to anger her in any way.

Many times as they captured various ships, Calico Jack would force the sailors from the captured ship to work for him. On one such occasion they had overtaken a Dutch merchant ship and one of the sailors was a handsome young man. Anne couldn't help herself, as her womanly feelings began to be drawn towards this young Dutch sailor. She knew what Calico Jack would do if he knew how she felt towards another man. As she approached the young sailor one evening, when all was quite and the young man was standing guard, Anne whispered to him that she was a woman. To her surprise, the young man turned out to be a woman herself. This was Mary Read. Anne was sworn to secrecy about Mary, but Captain Jack felt that she was growing to close to this young Dutch sailor, and through a fit of jealousy he wanted to put him to death. Anne had to inform him that this young sailor was also a woman. Both Anne and Mary fought hard all the time they were with Calico Jack. One night, as they lay at anchor in Dry Harbor Bay while the men were drunk, Captain Barnet pulled up alongside of them. Calico Jack, with the help of Anne and Mary, fought hard to hold the ship. His men were to drunk to fight, and most of them tried to find places to hide. Mary, in a fit of rage fired her pistol into the group of drunks. She killed one man, while injuring others, but it was to no avail. The battle was soon over, and they were all taken prisoner. Anne and Mary were spared from being hung, because they were both pregnant.

Calico Jack was granted the opportunity to see Anne before he was executed. Anne just told him that if he had fought like a man, he would not have had to be hung like a dog. These were the words that followed Captain Calico Jack Rackam as he went to meet the hangman.

Katelyn was thrilled by what she had read about Anne Bonney and Mary Read. She could hardly wait to study piracy in depth. She would take the books to work with her, and if it wasn't to busy, she could continue her study.

Although it turned out to be quite busy at the motel that evening, Katelyn got very little reading in, but she couldn't help but let her mind wander a bit. She couldn't imagine piracy being romantic, but surly Anne and Mary must have had feelings for their men. Mary had fallen in love with a sailor who she married according to pirates laws.

After Captain Jack's ship had been captured Mary's lover was released, because he convinced the Judge that Captain Rackam had forced him to join to the task. Mary must have been happy that her lover was once more a free man. Mary died of sickness before she could give birth to her baby. Anne had her baby and then because of the plea from the Jamaicans who knew her father, she was allowed to return home to be with her father.

Katelyn finished her shift and went home. She had a hard time not opening the books that night, but she managed to convince herself to sleep first. There would be plenty of time for her to read after she got up in the morning. She lay awake for a long time thinking about what it would have been like being a pirate woman. All those men cursing and swearing at one another. All those drunken brawls they encountered from being out to sea to long.

As sleep finally swept over her, Katelyn was dreaming of big white sails filled and driven by the wind. The mighty ship pushing its way towards the waves that came at her, lifted her bow high out of the waters as each wave crashed into her. Katelyn was standing at the front of the bow rising and falling as each new wave threatened to send her over backwards. The ocean spray felt cool as it washed over her face. Then, the waves stopped and the ship lay still in the waters. A hand brushed against hers, and she turned to see Rolland standing behind her. His hand was stretched out beckoning her to come to him.

Quickly stepping away from the railing, Katelyn smiled as Rolland placed his arms around her. She had enjoyed riding the waves, but now that the sea was calm, there was no other place she would rather be than in Rolland's arms. They walked over to Rollands quarters as Katelyn's heart raced. Finally she was going to experience the ultimate. As the waves of the ocean had lifted the bow of the ship out of the water, waves of ecstasy lifted her emotions out of control.

The door opened as Rolland pushed against it. His bed seemed to beckon to them. Katelyn thought her heart would burst as she was filled with anticipation of Rollands next move. The door closed behind them, and they were all alone. As their lips touched, fire works went off inside of Katelyn, and then she sat up in bed screaming, "No, we can't."

Looking around in the dark. Katelyn realized where she was, and she sighed as she lay back in bed. How strange it felt to think that even though she hadn't read but a little about pirates, she still romanticised about them. Then, as usual, nothing happened.

"Oh Rolland," Katelyn was a bit frusterated, "Why don't you ask me to marry you?"

She closed her eyes and was asleep within fifteen minutes. Her dreams were not quite as dramatic as the first one that night, but she still dreamt of being out on the ocean on a gigantic sailing ship. It was the biggest ship that Katelyn had ever seen, and no other ship could touch it. Then of course, Rolland was her captain, and there was none like him in the whole world.

In the morning, Katelyn made herself some breakfast, and then she sat down in her comfortable chair to read. She read about Blackbeard, and William Kidd who were both ruthless men. Neither one of them had any feelings for other human beings. William Kidd was hanged in England for piracy and murder. Stories had it that Kidd buried much treasure in different locations, but there wasn't enough substantial evidence to support these stories.

Katelyn was more interested in the history of the famous pirate Jean Lafitte. He was supposed to be a very handsome and romantic man. A real ladies man, one of the books had said. He had started out to sea at a very young age, but he learned well and fast everything there was to know about sailing ships. After quarrelling with the captain of the ship, Lafitte had abandoned ship and taken up with some privateers. They soon realized the amount of knowledge Lafitte had, and they made him captain. Lafitte began to rob and plunder other ships, and from there he started to make a name for himself. All the booty that they gathered from captured ships was taken to Barrataria, on the coast of Louisiana, where they would be sold at auction held there by the pirates. People from all parts of Lower Louisiana would come and buy at these auctions even knowing that they were smuggled goods from captured ships.

Katelyn dreamed of Rolland being Jean Lafitte, and she was the woman who loved him. Her name was Linnea McDowell whose father was a very wealthy merchantman. Mr. McDowell did not like the idea of his daughter going to these pirate auctions, but she would go to them anyway, because she was in love with Jean Lafitte. Whenever he was there, he would shower Linnea with gifts of renown beauty. Just being near him caused her heart to melt. Although Lafitte was a pirate, he was such a gentleman, and the other woman envied Linnea.

Word had come to Linnea that Jean had arrived in port, but her father had also heard the news. Knowing where she was off to, he stopped her as she headed for the door. McDowell loathed the idea that his daughter was seeing a pirate. His high classed friends had also seen her with that man. It bothered McDowell that his daughter would rather spend time with such scum than to be with her own kind.

"Linnea," McDowell spoke sternly, "I don't want to see you going to that filthy auction today."

"Father," Linnea loved her father, but she hated his control on her life, "I am twenty-three years of age, and am old enough to know what I want."

"What you want!" McDowell exclaimed. "Child, you are hanging around with worthless trash."

"They might be trash to you, Father," Linnea was angry at her father for calling Jean trash, "But to me they are my friends."

"Linnea! How can you say that?" Mcdowell blurted out. "Don't you care what people are saying about you?"

"I think you are more concerned about your name than you are about me," Linnea snickered.

"You aren't using your head, child."

"Don't you worry about me, Father," Linnea patted him on the arm. "I'll look after myself, while you sit with all your stuffy friends who don't even know what life is all about."

Linnea left before her father could say more. He sputtered something, but she didn't catch what he said. As she headed for the street, some of the people looked at her in disgust. They knew where she was going, because everybody heard when there was a pirate ship in port. None of the high classed people approved of such auctions, and they were trying to get the governor to put a stop to them.

With head held up with dignity, Linnea headed for the open field near the port where the auction was being held. It didn't matter to her what her father's friends thought. After all, they didn't even know what real living was. They figured that daily tea parties is what the women should attend, while the men made their fortunes. Linnea was proud of Jean Lafitte for robbing from these high classed ships, and the bringing the goods in for auction.

All her life, Linnea had been dragged from party to party with the high classed people, and it had always bored her to tears. She wanted adventure in her life, and when she had come across Jean Lafitte, her whole life seemed to change. These people knew how to live. Maybe robbing wasn't nice, but then, some of these stiff necked people like her own father needed to be cut down a bit. Their minds were filled with ways to get more riches. Were they, in their greed, any better than those buccaneers who robbed from the rich to become rich themselves. Although they plundered ships, their life was not easy as they fought gale forced winds that threatened to tear the ship apart. Fighting each ship, they plundered, was not an easy task, and outrunning battle ships, from the Queens Navy, was always a challenge. Linnea's father, and those like him, never faced such challenges.

Linnea's mother had died when she was sixteen, and after that her father had raised her by sending her to a fancy boarding school. Her mother had desired for years to see the day that father would finally say that he had enough money so he could settle down. The more money father made, the farther away he seemed to get. All he cared about was to be seen with the high classed people.

Mother had not been that way. Although she enjoyed dressing well, she just wanted her husband by her side. Even on the day she died, Father had been to busy making money to be by her side. Linnea had been there for her mother, and her last words to Linnea were, "My Darling Linnea. Please find yourself a man that enjoys life."

From that day on, Linnea had promised herself not to get involved with men of high esteem. While she was in boarding school, she would dream of the day when the right man would sweep her off her feet and take her away where life was not so complicated.

Many times, rich young sophisticated men would try to court her, but she would flatly refuse them. At first her father had been upset by such behaviour, but in time he stopped trying to get Linnea to change.

"You're just like your mother," he had said one day.

That angered Linnea, because all her mother ever wanted was to have a family life that was not congested with high minded people constantly invading her home. She had followed McDowell only because she wanted to keep peace in the family.

Already years before she passed away, her love for the man she married had gone out. He had been a dashing and daring young man when she first met him. His ambition had intrigued her, because she knew he could make it no matter what he did. Fame and fortune had stifled his brain. His goal in life had been to become rich so as never to see his family suffer. He had become rich alright, but yet his family suffered. Mrs. McDowell had stayed with him, for him, not for her.

These thoughts plagued Linnea as she walked down towards the docks. She wasn't interested in the auction. There was only one thing she wanted, and that was to see the man that stole her heart. If anyone should steal her heart, she figured it should be a thief.

Lafitte would still be on board the ship, because he would want to make sure that everything was in place in case they needed to slip away rather quickly. He had not lived a successful life as a pirate by being unprepared. He would stay with the ship till every detail had been looked after. They would need more supplies and ammunition, as well, the men would have to make sure the ship was clean. Although he was a pirate, Lafitte believed in keeping a clean ship.

When Linnea neared the docks, her reddish hair gleamed in the sunlight, and although her beauty dazzled the men as she walked, they all knew that she was Lafitte's women. No one dared touch Linnea for fear that Lafitte would run him through with his sword. They stepped aside to let her go by, but that didn't stop their mouth from watering.

Lafitte was looking towards the dock through a spy glass just as Linnea approached the end of the dock. One of the sailors offered to row her out to the ship, but she politely refused. Now that Jean had seen her, he would come to shore to greet her properly. Waving in recognition of her, Lafitte quickly climbed down the rope ladder that hung alongside the ship. Entering a boat that was moored at the end of the ladder, he proceeded to row towards shore.

Linnea's heart beat faster with each stroke of the paddle. If only her father could be half the man that Jean was, she thought, then maybe he would be easier to get along with. She didn't hate her father, but the way he had been towards her mother left a bad taste in her mouth. All the riches in the world could never replace the love she had for Jean Lafitte.

As the boat came alongside the dock, Linnea thought her heart would leap out of her chest. It had been two months since she had seen Jean, all the while her heart had longed for his return. Jean stepped out of the boat and threw the line to one of the men standing there.

"Tie her up mate," he ordered as the rough looking man grabbed the rope.

"With pleasure Mr. Lafitte," he spoke assuredly.

Smiling at Linnea, he reached out to take her in his arms, then changed his mind. It had been a long time since he had been able to bathe. Lafitte knew that he would smell of sweat and hard work. He desired to take Linnea in his arms, but he needed to get cleaned up first.

"Linnea my Darling," Lafitte smiled at her as he admired her radiant beauty, "I desire to hold you in my arms, but I must visit the bath house first."

"Nonsense, My Love," Linnea laughed at Lafitte. "I'll have you the way you are."

Suddenly, Linnea's arms were about his neck. She didn't care if he smelled a bit. If only her father could be as considerate as the man she loved. Her father always smelled fresh and clean, but that didn't win any popularity votes from her. At least Jean cared enough for Linnea to think about how he appeared in front of her. Her father only cared how people would judge his appearance. He dressed so that others would praise him for his lot in society.

"Honey," Linnea was almost in tears, "I've missed you so much that I don't care if you didn't bathe yet."

"Linnea Darling," Lafitte smiled at her, "Your beauty is breath taking. I hate to dirty such beauty."

"Beauty is in the heart," Linnea replied.

"Yes," Jean continued to admire her, "But I would like to be clean so that I might be more presentable to you."

"Alright Jean," Linnea taunted him, "I guess I can let you get cleaned up."

"Why don't you go over to the auction and wait for me there," Lafitte suggested. "If there is something there that you desire to have, I'll get it for you."

Linnea agreed, so she wandered about the auction area admiring all the booty that was being sold. This was goods taken off English and Spanish merchant ships. These two countries hated Lafitte because he always managed to slip away from their battle ships. Wherever their battle ships went, Lafitte was not to be found, and if found, he always managed to outrun them. It was as though he knew where they would be at all times.

While Linnea looked over the goods to be auctioned, she couldn't help but smile. Some rich sophisticated people had been relieved of their burden. Maybe someone should also relieve her father of that burden. After all, he never seemed to have time for real living, and without realizing he was doing it, he wanted to forbid Linnea of having a life. She was about to pick up an interesting looking embroidered shawl with beads, when suddenly her fathers coach pulled up beside her.

The door opened, and her father stuck his head out and ordered, "Get in the coach Linnea."

Linnea spoke with indignity, "I prefer to stay here Father."

Nonsense child," McDowell retorted.

"What do you know about nonsense?" Linnea taunted her father as she continued to examine the shawl with admiration.

"This is all stolen goods," McDowell was annoyed at his daughters behaviour. "You are hanging around with thieves."

"Father," Linnea put down the shawl and turned to face him, "This is not stolen goods. Somebody just got a burden relieved from off their shoulders."

"What are you saying child?" McDowell demanded.

"If someone were to relieve you of some of your burden, maybe you to could start too live." Linnea fought hard to hold back the words she really wanted to say, because she was furious inside.

"You are babbling like a fool child," McDowell was astonished at what his daughter was saying. "Now climb into this coach and we can be on our way."

"I'm not coming with you Father," Linnea stared at him in disbelief. Couldn't her father see that she didn't want to associate with his kind.

"Linnea," McDowell was angry, "You get in here right this minute."

"When will you get it through your head, Father, that I don't want to hang around with your kind of scum," Linnea glared at him.

People were beginning to look in their direction, so McDowell lowered his voice as he continued. "I tried to give you a good life-------------"

Linnea cut him off, "Like the life you gave Mother,' she laughed mockingly as she threw her arms in the air. "This is life, Father."

"Now look here child," McDowell couldn't believe what he heard his daughter saying, "I gave your mother everything she could ask for."

"Except for the love and affection she deeply desired from you Father," Linnea turned and walked away as tears welled up in her eyes.

"Linnea," McDowell called out, "Linnea, don't you turn your back on me."

Without another word to her father, Linnea disappeared into the crowd. She needed to dry her tears before Jean came back. 'He must never know the way Father is,' she thought. Although she was against her father's ways, she still didn't want Jean Lafitte or anyone else to snuff out his life. Linnea hoped that someday her father would come to realize the truth about money. What good was money if you never spent time with your loved ones. Money was okay to have, as long as the money didn't have you. Father spent very little time at home, because he was always to busy making the money that was ruining his life.

She was startled back to reality as a hand gently touched her arm, and a voice that she recognized as Jeans, said, "Linnea Darling! You seem to be far off somewhere."

"I'm sorry Jean," Linnea felt bad that she had let her father's life interfere with her happiness at seeing Jean again. "I was just deep in thought."

Lafitte spun her around so that they were looking eye to eye. The affect of the tears were still plainly visible. Gently placing his hands on her face, Lafitte began to stroke her cheeks with his thumbs. He was not a man to pry into someone else's affairs, but because he loved Linnea, he didn't want to see her hurt. Lafitte would kill anyone who harmed the woman he hoped to marry someday.

"Linnea Darling! Who hurt you?" He demanded of her.

"It's okay Honey," she tried to smile reassuringly. "I'm just so happy to see you. It seems like such a long time since we were together. I hate to see you go."

"Well Linnea Darling," Lafitte leaned down and placed a kiss on her lips, "Soon I hope to be able to stay around for longer periods of time."

"Why! Do you plan to quit what you are doing?" Linnea questioned.

"I have enough things stored away that I don't have to go out all the time." Lafitte laughed at Linnea's questioning expression.

"Don't tease me Jean," Linnea looked longingly at him.

"I have enough captains under me right now that I could give my orders from a house that I bought not too far from here." Lafitte did his best to assure Linnea that he was telling the truth.

"Oh Honey," Linnea was beside herself with joy, "That would be wonderful to have you around all the time."

"Linnea Darling," Lafitte laughed heartily, "I would still be going out from time to time. Can't become rusty now you know."

CHAPTER EIGHT

LAFITTE TOOK LINNEA OUT for a classy dinner where the high rollers, like her father, ate. As they sat and talked, Lafitte shared about the adventures he encountered as they plundered the Spanish and British ships. He laughed heartily as he expressed how much he loved to relieve those rich Spaniards and British of their burden of lucre. Of course, the Spanish and British didn't think to lightly of what these so called renegades were doing.

Suddenly, Linneas father entered the dinning room. He was about to follow the host to his usual table when he spotted Linnea with Lafitte. His blood vessels were ready to explode as the red rose from his neck to his face. How dare that varmint take his daughter to dine at the place for upper class people. The nerve of that rogue to use profits from stolen goods to dine his lovely daughter. He would put a stop to this nonsense immediately before Linnea took this to far. Excusing himself, to the host, he headed for his daughters table Lafitte, knowing who Linneas father was, saw him approach their table. He stood up and bowed his head in the most humble way. Pointing to one of the two extra chairs set around the table, he politely inquired of McDowell if he cared to join them.

"Monsieur McDowell! Would you care to grace us with your presence by joining us for dinner tonight?" Lafitte spoke loudly so that his voice carried throughout the dinning room.

"Lafitte," McDowell was taken back by the man's polite mannerism and it angered him even more. "I didn't come here to join the likes of you for dinner."

"Well Monsieur," Lafitte continued to be polite. "What is it that I could do for you?"

McDowell was beside himself. The politeness of Lafitte seemed to cut him to the core like a hot knife cutting butter. He was at loss what to say, but his anger towards this man got the best of him as he yelled at Lafitte, "How dare you come into this place."

People were looking in their direction to see what the commotion was all about. McDowell felt uneasy as this situation was not going the way he had expected it to. He was well known and respected among the upper class society, and now he felt at a loss with this renegade mocking him with politeness

"Monsieur," Lafitte tried to sound sincere as he sensed McDowells uneasiness "Is this not a good place to take a beautiful young lady to dine and dance."

"That young lady happens to be my daughter," McDowell snapped back with rage. "I don't want to see her with the likes of you."

"I'm sorry Monsieur," Lafitte took full advantage of the situation, "I do believe that your daughter is old enough to decide who she wants to dine with."

There were a few snickers around the room, but nobody came to McDowells aid. Had he left well enough alone, he would not be in this predicament. Lafitte was well able to handle himself in any given situation, and this proved it. He was a pirate, but when it came to Linnea, or whenever in a public place, he was a gentleman. Although most of his life was spent on board a ship, Lafitte had not come this far by being ignorant of the ways of people from every walk of life.

Linnea felt a bit sorry for her father, but at the same time she relished the thought to see him squirm in the tantalizing grip Lafitte had on his arrogant attitude. He was making a complete fool of himself, while Jean calmly spun a web around him. It was time that her father was taken down off his high horse and brought to realize that fame and fortune meant nothing to Linnea if it came at the expense of others. Yes, Lafitte plundered ships for their booty, but he never assaulted any American ships, or those of less fortune. It was the Pious people like her own father who lost out to the mighty Lafitte. Most of the people of Barrataria left Lafitte alone because he didn't bother them. McDowell on the other hand was one of those who was a self appointed important man.

"You are in here under false pretenses," McDowell spit out vehemently. "Your riches come from stolen goods. You never earned one penny of the money you possess."

"Monsieur," Lafitte smiled mockingly at McDowell. "I assure you that none of the money that I have ever came from your pocket. Besides, have you ever tried to plunder one of those rich English or Spanish galleons. I assure you Monsieur it is not an easy task."

"I'll see you hang for your devious assaults on innocent ships," McDowell blurted out.

"Now, now, Monsieur," Lafitte laughed heartily at the expense of McDowells uncertainty in this situation as he he tried hard to get the upper hand. "You must get a hold of yourself. Your friends are laughing at your foolish behaviour and your senseless babble."

Overwhelmed by anger and embarrassment at not being able to bring Lafitte down, McDowell turned and headed towards the door, changing his mind about eating in this place. He had never in his whole life been as humiliated as he had been that evening. This piece of trash that called himself a man had managed not only to plunder ships, but he had also stolen his daughters heart. Why couldn't she see through this renegade.

Lafitte couldn't help but put in one last word for good measure. He knew how Linnea despised the lifestyle of her father. She had shared with him how her mother had desired some romantic affection instead of all the glamour McDowells money had bought her. Linnea could still hear her mother with her dying breath begging Linnea to find a real man, not someone who thrived on prestige. Although McDowell was well known and respected as a businessman, Lafitte also had his admirers.

"Monsieur," Lafitte called out as McDowell was about to close the door, "You didn't join us for dinner. What a pity! I was even going to pay."

The other diners snickered as McDowell made a hasty retreat through the door without looking back. They knew what kind of man Lafitte was, but to most of the women, Lafitte was a handsome, romantic, rough and tough go get them type of man. Although most of these women despised her for going to the auctions, they envied Linnea, and fantasized having a romantic love affair with Lafitte, even though they were married. To the men, Lafitte wasn't bothering them, even though they rejected piracy, as long as he robbed from the British and Spanish ships, they didn't mind that he enjoyed dinner with Linnea in this high classed place. They had to agree with Lafitte, Linnea was old enough to make up her own mind, even if she desired to be with a pirate. After all, Lafitte wasn't hurting them by raiding the British and Spanish ships. Each to their own, so to speak. Nobody made decisions without reaping the consequences, whether good or bad.

After dining and dancing, Lafitte walked with Linnea on the beach along the shore, in the cool of the night. As the moon glittered on the water, and the waves splashed against the shoreline, gently spraying salt water into the air, Linnea's heart throbbed in her chest. She desired so much to be the wife of Jean Lafitte, but it also scared her. What if he never came back from one of his raiding excursions? It made her shudder to think of such a thing happening.

Lafitte seeing Linnea shudder, inquired of her, "What is it My Darling Linnea? Are you cold?"

"I was just thinking of you out there plundering, and then maybe someday not coming back to me," she replied.

"My Darling Linnea," Lafitte laughed, "I'll always come back to you."

Linnea stopped and whirling around to face him, she looked directly into his eyes and spoke with concern. "How can you be so sure, My Love?"

"Oh Darling Linnea," Lafitte gently wrapped his arms around her and placed a kiss on her lips before continuing. "I have out witted, out thought, out run, and out fought every ship we have come in contact with. You have nothing to worry about."

"That is easy for you to say Jean," Linnea was almost in tears, "I love you and when you are gone, I always fear you won't return to me."

Without another word, as the moon kept glimmering off the water, and the waves continued to spray the air with a fine mist of salt water, Lafitte pulled Linnea close to his own body. The thrilling deep desire of making love to this man, ravaged her body like fire brands that threatening to consume her. Her supple breasts stiffened, while her heart throbbed with anticipation as Lafitte's kisses caressed her lips, and then slowly moved down her neckline. Her hormones were screaming with jubilation as she was lost in the bliss of the moment, oblivious to her surroundings. Then, they were both lying on the sand of the beach lost in each others embrace.

Although every fiber in Linnea's body screamed for more, she suddenly realized that they were not in a very good situation. Releasing her hold on Jean she pushed herself away from him. "My Love," her breath came out in gasps, "I desire to have you, but this way is not the right way."

Lafitte, also breathing heavily didn't rebuke Linnea for shoving away from him. "Darling Linnea, I'm sorry for almost taking advantage of you."

"It's okay My Love," she smiled in the darkness as they picked themselves off the beach. "I desired to go all the way with you tonight, but realized in the nick of time that this would not be a good idea."

As they walked along the shore line, both deep in thought about what had almost happened, Lafitte couldn't help but admire Linnea even more. He would never intentionally set out to hurt her. Her desire was to wait till marriage before giving her body to any man. Laffite respected her for her decision, and being the gentleman he was, praised her for her commitment.

When they reached the street, Lafitte hired a couch to take Linnea home. He bade her goodnight and reassured her that next time he was in port, he would see her again. He watched till the darkness swallowed up the coach from sight before making his way back to his ship, where the men would be waiting to set sail for more adventure. He laughed as he rowed toward the ship, about how Linnea had realized in the nick of time that they were together on a sandy beach, oblivious to their surroundings, passionately embraced in each others love. Soon, he promised himself, he would marry Linnea and give her the life she deserved, but now he had more ships to plunder.

CHAPTER NINE

LAFITTE KEPT COMING AND going, but every time he anchored at Barrataria he spent most of his time with Linnea. He left the auctioning to his crew, not even caring if they cheated him or not. His deepest desire was to be near the woman that he loved. Linnea had pleaded with him a number of times to let her go with him on his ship, but he wouldn't hear of it. Although he had a good crew of brigands, he couldn't trust them to keep their hands off his lady. Besides, it would be too dangerous when they fought with other ships.

One day, Lafitte received word from the British that they wanted to declare war against Louisiana, and that they would pay Lafitte handsomely if he should join forces with them. Lafitte informed them that he would get back to them in a couple days. This gave him time to inform the governor of the state what was taking place, and to make a deal with him about a pardon for every buccaneer who signed up to fight against the British. The pardon was agreed upon with a letter from the President pardoning every renegade that would fight for the United States of America.

Lafitte showed the pardon to every man, and they accepted the pardon in exchange for their willingness to help defend Louisiana. The men would serve under General Jackson, nicknamed Stoneface, because of his seriousness. The battle was hot, and many men gave their life for their country, but the British had to retreat and declare defeat. Lafitte's men had fought hard, and because they were well seasoned men for battle, they could now hold their head up high as free men.

Linnea feared for Lafitte as he went to battle the British. She knew how they hated Lafitte, and after turning down their proposal, they had become even more hateful towards the man who had plundered their ships. Lafitte was good when he was out in the water, but could he also conquer his foe on land. Her father, who although he loved his daughter, still despised the man she insisted on seeing. He hoped that Lafitte would meet his end while out on the battlefield.

When the battle was over, Linnea reminded her father that it was Lafitte who had helped to win the war. He of course, insisted that it could have been done without that pirates help. Little did McDowell know that if it hadn't been for Lafitte's ammunition the war would have been lost. As they were running low, Lafitte had approached General Jackson and volunteered the use of his own supplies which had been taken from many plundered ships. How could Jackson disagree with such a proposal? Taking a few men with him, Lafitte had retreated through the swamp land and then returned with the means of winning the war. He had become a hero, but, although many of his men enjoyed their freedom, Lafitte couldn't settle down. With a great number of his old crew, he set out to sea and sailed to Galveston Bay, Texas, because Barrataria was no longer a place where pirates could be safe. Although he continued his piracy, Lafitte also became the Governor of Galveston.

Linnea cried till her eyes were red when she heard that Lafitte had fled out to sea. Laffite had been unable to see Linnea before his retreat, because he was being sought for on land and sea. She wasn't sure where he had gone, but she did know that it was no longer safe for him here. He had refused his pardon, thus making him a fugitive of the state. If only he had come to take her with him, she would have gone no matter what the cost. Her father wasn't changing, and it seemed the more money he possessed, the worse he became. He would be better off dead, she thought to herself. All that stinking money was nothing else than grief. She had begun to hate him when he had told her that he hoped Lafitte would die during the battle against the British war ships. When Lafitte had fled to the sea, after refusing his pardon, McDowell had laughed and reminded Linnea of the worthless scum Lafitte was.

Lafitte longed for Linnea to be in his arms. Many nights he lay awake thinking of her, but he couldn't bring himself to agree that she should be with him as long as his life was constantly being threatened. The day came that he couldn't take it anymore, so with a handful of his trustworthy seamen, he set sail for Barrataria. They slid silently into her port in the middle of the night. While he slipped off to shore with two other men to row the boat, he had ordered the others to make a hasty retreat if he wasn't back by morning.

Leaving the two men with the boat, he also told them to leave by morning if he didn't return. Slipping quietly along the dark streets, he finally came in sight of the McDowell Mansion. McDowell had built a high wall all around the place, but because Lafitte was used to the ways of the sea, he had no problem scaling the wall. Once over on the inside, he had to examine the place for the whereabouts of Linnea's room. There was a light on in one of the upper rooms, so Lafitte decided to wait in the shadows till the light was extinguished. As he watched the window, he suddenly saw a silhouette of a woman behind the curtain. Was this Linnea, or could it be one of the servants still walking about at this hour of the night. Then, without warning, the light was snuffed out and the silhouette disappeared along with it. Not wanting to lose anymore time, Lafitte gathered up some small stones. He had to cross the courtyard before he was close enough to the Mansion to throw the stones at the widow where the light had been. As he drew near, he knew he couldn't afford any mistakes. Taking a stone in his right hand, he tossed it at the window. There was no response, so he repeated the process, prepared for a hasty retreat in case his guess was wrong and this was not Linnea's room This time he heard the window opening, and the head that looked down into the courtyard was that of Linnea. The moon shone through the trees and the beams fell upon her beautiful head.

"My Darling Linnea," Lafitte spoke softly but yet loud enough for her to hear. "I have come to take you away with me."

Linneas heart was ready to burst as she heard Lafitte's voice in the courtyard. She was so excited that the words she wanted to express wouldn't come out. She let out a squeal of gratitude before her head disappeared from sight. It wasn't long before she came dashing towards Lafitte, in her night gown. She had not even stopped to get dressed. When Lafitte embraced her, he could feel her heart beating while he pressed her body tightly against his own. As their lips met, he gently lifted her off the ground, and he began spinning around with Linnea in his arms. He suddenly felt pain ripping through his body as he heard an explosion.

Neither one of them had seen McDowell coming out of the house. While they were engaged in kissing, McDowell had fired a shot at Lafittes back. His aim had been off a bit, and the ball had just grazed Lafitte's side as it glanced off his belt. Although it was painful, and it hadn't split the skin, the rib felt like it was cracked.

Drawing his sword, Lafitte moved slowly towards McDowell, angered by the thought that McDowell would shoot at him while Linnea was in his arms. The fool was not too bright, or else he had been too sure of himself. Besides the fact that he could have shot his own daughter, he had only brought one shot with him, and had not even brought a sword. Lafitte had all intentions of running his own sword right through the man. Such a coward that would stoop so low as to shoot a man in the back had no right to live. Pain or no pain, Lafitte decided that tonight this man would die.

"McDowell," Lafitte snarled, "Be prepared to meet your maker tonight." Gone was the politeness he had shown this man before. Now he was out for revenge.

"You can't kill me Lafitte," McDowell pleaded. "I'm not armed."

"What about that gun you have in your hand?" Lafitte questioned?

McDowell had forgotten that he still held the gun. Tossing it to the ground, he held his hands up in the air. He had been a fool to try and kill this man, but he had also thought that only one ball would finish him off. Lafitte had moved just as McDowell squeezed off the trigger, and now he realized that this could be the end. It suddenly dawned on him, he could have shot his own daughter.

"Linnea," McDowells voice quivered, "Don't let this man kill me!"

"Why don't you use your riches to set you free Father?" Linnea taunted.

"Don't be silly girl," McDowell spoke with uncertainty, "Money isn't any good in this situation."

Lafitte was enjoying the sight of McDowell squirming in the last moments of his life. Let him squirm and feel fear, he thought. McDowell will know with his last breath that all those years of hoarding money couldn't even buy him life. His whole life's ambition had been to obtain as much money as he could, only to find out that he had wasted a lifetime of real living.

"Lafitte," McDowell could back up no farther, because he had bumped into a wall, "I don't believe for one minute that a man of your stature would kill a defenceless man."

"Shut up! McDowell!" Lafitte couldn't stand a whimpering man pleading for life. In all the years that he had fought, every man Lafitte had been in combat with, had done it bravely. Now he was facing a snivelling coward who had all his life depended upon money to get him through.

"I'll give you all that I own," McDowell tried to barter for his life.

"What do I want with your money you imbecile," Lafitte jeered at him.

"You always rob from the rich," McDowell continued to postpone his death.

"I'm not interested in money, you old fool," Lafitte snapped at him.

"Then why do you rob?" McDowell hoped to talk his way through this mess.

"To cut down scum like you who think that money can buy anything. You put your daughter through hell because you were too busy building empires. Then you have the guts to judge a man of my stature. If it wasn't for my kind of people, you would be under British rule today. While we fought for freedom, what were you doing?" Lafitte was angered by the thought of this rich scumbag sitting idly by while many of his own men had died for this man's freedom.

Lafitte suddenly lunged forward and plunged his sword into McDowells mid section. With a scream of horror, McDowell looked at his daughter as he sank to his knees. Life was fast slipping away from him, and he couldn't even think of one good thing he had done in the time that he was alive. Even his own daughter hadn't stopped this renegade from plunging his sword into him. McDowell looked at Linnea as she held onto Lafitte.

There was no remorse in her eyes. Was that a smile he saw on her face? Was she happy to see him die this way?

"Linnea," McDowell called out to her.

Linnea couldn't move. Even though she loved her father, and he was dying right before her eyes, she still couldn't help feeling relieved that she would soon be free from all this man's riches and wealth. McDowell never showed real love to her or to her mother. They were only part of his possessions, and now he could no longer try to control and manipulate her. When her mother had died, Linnea had wished that she could die with her.

McDowell toppled over on his side. Blood was spilling out of his mouth, and yet he tried to talk, but no words came forth. Nobody would ever know what McDowell had tried to say before he died. He had tried to gain the whole world, while losing his own soul. He must have thought he would live forever, because he never made out a will. Linnea never got to see any of the wealth that McDowell had accumulated over the years, but she didn't mind. What she wanted out of life was a man that loved and cared for her, and that is what she had found in Jean Lafitte.

The town had to bury McDowell, because Linnea had just walked away and left the dead body lying in the courtyard. She went with Lafitte to the boat that was still waiting for them.

After boarding the ship, Lafitte ordered his crew to manoeuver her quietly out to sea. They made it back safely to Galveston where Lafitte gave Linnea a nice cabin overlooking the bay. That way she could always see the ships coming and going.

Word reached Lafitte that his fleet of ships was being taken one at a time and that there was no mercy shown to the men of these ships. Procuring a large and fast brigantine, Lafitte set sail with all intentions of robbing not only British and Spanish ships, but ships from all nations. He was angry with America for waging war against his ships. Lafitte had never plundered any American ships, but yet they now were after him and his men.

As they plundered the sea, the British caught wind that Lafitte himself was back in operation. One of the British war ships came upon Lafitte and throughout the heated battle, they managed to board Lafitte's brigantine. At this point, Lafitte was wounded two times, once from a grape shot which broke his leg, and he received a cut in the abdomen which caused him to bleed to death. Although

Lafitte had been a man of courage, strength, and he had great knowledge, he was marked as a man with crimes of the deepest kind.

Linnea insisted that Lafitte be buried behind the cabin overlooking the bay. It was very heartbreaking for her, because Jean Lafitte had asked her to marry him as he got into the boat that would take him to the brigantine. Like always, he was certain that he would return. The one man who she had always loved deeply would never be forgotten. Although others may think bad of the deeds he had done, Linnea would remember him as the man who relieved the rich from that life destroying thing called wealth. Lafitte had left all his possessions to Linnea in a will he had made out just prior to his last departure. It was not like the wealth her father had acquired before his death, but Linnea was happy to know that she could at least live long enough to enjoy what Lafitte had left behind for her.

CHAPTER TEN

KATELYN WAS CRYING AS she came out of her dream about Lafitte and Linnea. How tragic that scene had been. Of course Katelyn realized that the story had been her own romantic dream, because the only thing she had found in the history books about his romantic life was that Lafitte had been a real ladies man. So Katelyn had just imagined Rolland to be Lafitte, and she was Linnea. She just made believe that Lafitte only had one lady in his life that he loved. One thing that she realized through studying about pirates was, she couldn't get away from dreaming about Rolland even in that kind of setting. Also, Linnea never did find out what real intimacy was like with Lafitte.

Katelyn sighed as she wiped away her tears. No matter how hard she tried to get into history that would not involve any romantic feelings, her love for Rolland naturally included him in her dreams. Her heart ached as she thought about being with Rolland the rest of her life.

The time that Rolland was gone seemed to fly by as long as Katelyn kept her nose buried in pirate books. The day after he returned Katelyn had her day off, so they went out for a wonderful dinner that evening. Rolland talked about what he had accomplished in his few days away in Victoria. He was excited that even if Katelyn was accepted at the museum in Victoria, he would probably be coming up there from time to time to work on the account he had established there and then he could concentrate on asking her to marry him, but until that time he would have to fight to hold off. Katelyn was excited about the bit of news that Rolland would be coming to Victoria from time to time, but in her heart she still cried out, 'Marry me you fool.' Katelyn told him that she had tried to keep her mind occupied with historical matters concerning pirates. Of course she left out the part about Rolland being Lafitte.

After they were done their dinner, they drove to Indian Battle Park and walked around. It felt good walking beside Rolland, and even though he had been gone a few days, Katelyn felt as though he had been near her all that time. 'The imagination is a wonderful thing,' she thought as she held Rolland's hand. She knew it was dangerous for them to be out alone so late at night, but she would just have to control her emotions.

Crossing under the High Level Bridge, they continued walking, following the nature paths, until they came to one of the picnic fire pits. It was already late in the evening with the sun beginning to set. Sitting down together on one of the benches, they faced the west and watched the sky as it became filled with different shades of pink, blue, and yellow. Neither one of them wanted to move as they savoured the darkness that was slowly surrounding them. They were both lost in their own thoughts about how wonderful it was to be together.

After a long period of silence, Katelyn was the first one to speak. She had been thinking about starting a fire in the pit, and then just enjoying Rolland's company as they watched the fire burn till there was nothing left but the embers.

"Honey," she whispered as if she was afraid some one beside Rolland might hear her. "Can we build a fire before it gets dark and sit here for a while watching the flames until the fire slowly burns out?"

"That is an excellent idea Sweetie," Rolland spoke as he got up to get some wood. "I have something that I've been meaning to ask you, and tonight is a good time for that."

Katelyn got up to help Rolland gather firewood, but he told her just to sit while he got the fire started. As Rolland went over to the wood bin, Katelyn let her mind drift off into the past. She was once again the native princess Pretty Bird, and Rolland was Running Wild. After much talk, Running Wild had persuaded the elders to let him sit in on one of the counsel meetings. This of course was not the way of the Blackfoot, but Running Wild had a cunning way about getting people to see things his way. He wanted to sit around the counsel fire helping decide important issues for the band, so this would be a good experience for him. He had been told by Red Crow that he was only there to listen and to observe. With the Small Pox epidemic slowly wiping out the elders, Red Crow admitted that at least one young brave should be allowed to participate in case no elders were left to counsel. Running Wild might also contract the dreaded Small Pox, but that was a chance they would have to take. Many tribes were signing treaties with the white man and Red Crow was thinking seriously about doing that same thing. Running Wild, being a young brave, might disagree but if it had to be done then it would be done before they were all wiped out.

Running Wild was such a handsome brave, Pretty Bird thought. In her own imagination she believed that Running Wild was a very wise counsel member, even though he was not yet an elder in the counsel. What did those elders know anyway she thought proudly. She desired deeply that this wonderful brave would someday take notice of her and take her into his own tepee as his wife. She longed for the day that she could make Running Wild the happiest brave that ever lived.

Upon returning with the wood, Rolland could tell that Katelyn was dreaming again, and it made him smile. 'She sure has an imagination,' he thought as he proceeded to start the fire. Rolland didn't know what Katelyn imagined, just that he knew she would let herself drift off into whatever time period she was thinking about.

Katelyn smiled as she watched Rolland build the fire. How she longed to be with him forever, sharing his life and being there in times of need. In her romantic imagination of Lafitte and Linnea, she never got the opportunity to be his forever, but with Rolland it would be different. Katelyn believed that the day would come where Rolland would propose to her. Now that he had a client in Victoria, maybe tonight would be the night. After all, he had said he wanted to ask her some thing.

The fire was dazzling as it burned with ever increasing intensity. The flames danced vigorously as they licked hungrily at the logs that Rolland had placed in the pit. Sitting together, they watched silently as the fire slowly ate away at the wood. Nothing in the whole world mattered now, because they had each other, and it was as though they were the only two people on the earth at that very moment.

Rolland looked at Katelyn, and saw the reflection of the flames glimmering on her face. "Sweetie," he spoke softly, "I know that it is your desire to live in Victoria, so I would like to ask you something."

"What is it Honey?" Katelyn's voice quivered a bit as she thought her heart would burst.

"What will happen to us when you leave?"

Katelyn's heart nearly sank as she heard the question. She had half expected Rolland to pop the big question, but instead he wanted to know what would happen when she left. She couldn't be angry, because Rolland would ask when he was ready, but yet it frustrated her. How could she ever close the life of Pretty Bird and Running Wild without being married herself.

"Rolland you silly man," Katelyn scolded him teasingly. "Do you love me?"

"Of course I love you Sweetie, but I don't want to loose you! When you are in Victoria, I will only see you once, possibly twice a year."

Katelyn thought about the Titanic movie, Rose never lost her love for Jack, she had just hidden it in her heart all those years. If Rolland didn't propose to her before she left for Victoria, she wouldn't stop loving him. Another thing, unless Rolland died like Jack did, they could still get married some day.

Looking directly into his eyes, Katelyn whispered, "Rolland, no matter what happens, I could never stop loving you."

"What are you talking about girl?" Rolland laughed. "No matter what happens! What is that all about?"

Katelyn blushed as she realized, to Rolland that might seem like a silly thing to say. She was glad that it was too dark for him to see her red face. She never shared with Rolland the romantic dreams she had about the two of them together. If he proposed to her, then she might let him in on her little secret. Until then, she would keep it hidden deep in her heart.

"Well you know," Katelyn used the shadows of darkness to hide her embarrassment, "If I get accepted in Victoria, you might want to move on."

"Sweetie," Rolland turned and looked directly into her eyes as the fire reflected from her face, "I will always love you. There could never be anyone else for me."

Katelyn felt like screaming at him, "Well then propose to me you fool." But she knew better then to push Rolland.

She just looked lovingly and longingly at the man she so deeply desired to have. He was looking back at her, and as their faces moved closer together, and their lips met, waves of passion engulfed both of them. Fireworks went off inside like thousands of lightening bolts and then they toppled off the bench onto the ground next to the fire pit. That abruptly ended the fireworks, as they felt embarrassed at what had just happened.

Sitting up, their breath escaping their lungs in short rapid gasps, while feeling silly over what had happened, they looked around to make sure no one had seen them fall off the bench. They got up, brushed the dust off their cloths, and looked sheepishly at each other before bursting into laughter.

"Honey," Katelyn spoke, her heart still throbbing, "Your kisses are electrifying."

"That comes from mixing two chemicals together," Rolland replied, "Yours and mine."

"I knew you were a wise councilman," Katelyn laughed.

"Councilman!" Rolland was puzzled.

"Honey," Katelyn smiled at him because of the expression on his face. "You had to have been there."

"What does that mean?" Rolland questioned her.

"Well Honey," Katelyn squeezed his hand, "Throw another log on the fire, and sit with me while I explain it to you."

Katelyn told him about her fantasy that she had while he was getting the fire going. How she had imagined him being the Indian Brave Running Wild and how he had convinced the councilmen to let him sit in on counsel. She told Rolland how she had been Pretty Bird the beautiful native girl who was madly in love with Running Wild, yet Running Wild never noticed her. They both laughed about it, and Rolland teased her about being a beautiful native princess.

As time went by, they talked about various things that interested them. The night was clear, and the stars seemed to be brighter on this particular night. Maybe it was because the love they had for each other brought out a clearer view of the stars. The moon shone through the trees shedding its silvery beams of light on the couple as they shared each other's company. Their talk really meant nothing to either of them, it was like heavenly music to hear the other's voice.

The fire in the pit had burned down to glowing embers so they rose up and went for a walk to the rivers edge. The moon sent threads of glimmering light on the water that lapped gently against the river bank as it flowed swiftly down stream. An owl gave an eerie hoot off in the trees some where. There was a slight breeze that rustled through the grass as the couple stood facing each other.

As Katelyn closed her eyes, her body quivered with emotion, while her breasts rose and fell in rhythm to her deep breathing. She thought back to her story of Linnea and Jean Lafitte. They had dined together, and then as the music played softly, Lafitte had taken her in his arms as they danced slowly around the room. Katelyn pictured herself in that setting with her lover Rolland, who of course was Lafitte. The music had sped up a bit, but it was still sweet. Her dress billowed out as Lafitte spun her around catching her in his strong arms. As they floated along the floor, Linnea looked longingly into Jeans eyes. Oh how she desired to be his wife for as long as they both should live.

Rolland smiled at Katelyn as he stood looking at her closed eyes. Her eye lids fluttered, and he wondered what it was she was dreaming about this time. He admired Katelyn for the vivid imagination that she had. Although he was aware that she didn't share everything with him about her dreams, he didn't pressure her about it. She would share with him what she wanted him to know.

Suddenly her body reeled and Rolland reached out to catch her, before she toppled over the embankment into the river. Katelyn opened her eyes and realized that she was in Rolland's arms next to the river. She laughed gleefully as she looked up into his astonished face. 'This man sure has an effect on me,' she thought as she brushed her lips across his. Rolland didn't want to frighten her, but he had to tell her that she almost slipped into the river.

"Sweetie," Rolland spoke softly to her, "You almost ended up in the river when you reeled sideways."

Katelyn laid her head on Rollands shoulder, thankful that he had saved her from that embarrassing fall. As he embraced her, the masculine aroma of his cologne made her wish that this time could last forever. If only Rolland would propose to her, then she would always be his and her dreams could become more of a reality.

Her mind drifted once more, with the picture changing from a ball room to a meadow filled with beautiful flowers. In the middle of all this beauty was a stage with a couple dancing on it. The band was off to one side playing a love song. The couple on the stage were Rolland and Katelyn. He was wearing an astounding white tuxedo, while Katelyn was arrayed in a beautiful white wedding gown with a long train that flowed and waved in tune with the music. She twirled and spun, floating as if she were a feather. Rolland would gently pull her back to himself before twirling her around again.

Katelyn's mind snapped back to the present as Rolland wrapped his arms around her. Although he had powerful arms, he held her ever so gently. As their lips touched, they became locked together in the passion of love. Katelyn dreamed of the scene in Titanic where Jack and Rose were in the back of the car.

Suddenly she wrenched herself free from Rollands arms her breath coming out in gasps. The scene of Jack and Rose in the back of the car caused her to realize that the fire of passion that burned deep inside her for Rolland was so strong that they might go all the way. The nipples on her breasts stood out firm like the pyramids of Egypt.

"What's wrong Sweetie!" Rolland spoke a bit shocked at her sudden behaviour.

"We need to go home," Katelyn's voice quivered as she spoke.

"Is it something I did!" Rolland was puzzled.

"No Honey," Katelyn managed to steady herself, "We have to stop before I can no longer say no to you. The agreement was that we would abstain from sex, and right now I don't think I could stop if we continue."

"You're right Sweetie," Rolland agreed. "I was desiring to really have all of you tonight, so this is a good time to leave the park."

When they drove to Katelyn's apartment, they laughed and teased each other, making small talk, while Katelyn's heart throbbed as she reflected the moment they nearly lost it, twice, in the park, that evening.

Suddenly the thought occurred to her, 'What if Rolland didn't ask her to marry him? She would never know what it would be like to be locked together with him in rapturous ecstasy.' Why couldn't he just ask her to marry him? What was he waiting for? If he asked her, she would even reconsider the thought of wanting to work in Victoria. If they accepted her, she would just say that something more important had come up. The man of her dreams asked her to marry him so she must decline the job at the museum.

While Rolland walked Katelyn to her door, he couldn't help but admire her for her strength. Tonight he had not been able to hold back, but yet in the nick of time, Katelyn had pulled free from his grasp. She was an amazing young lady, and Rolland was happy to have her in his life. He knew that at the right time he would ask her to marry him, and then if she accepted, which he was quite sure she would, they could live their lives together in eternal bliss, but first he must respect her desire to fulfill the dream of her life. To interfere with that dream could be more devastating than refraining from proposing at this time. Waiting would most likely prove more beneficial in the end.

Rolland had fought hard to achieve his degree in accounting and his efforts had paid off as he quickly moved up the ladder of success. At his young age, the firm was sending him on trips all over, getting new clients, and helping those they already had acquired. Giving in to the cry of his hormones could be a disaster for his and Kaitlyn's future. In college many of the students had caroused and just drifted through their courses, believing they could make up time later. They decided it was more important to have fun while they were still young. Although many thought Rolland was crazy for not enjoying his youth, he had come out on top of the class with no regrets of not having fun. Many of his colleagues, who had breezed through college having fun, didn't even have a job in the field they had studied for. Rolland knew that Kaitlyn had also made many sacrifices to get the degree she had in history. The sacrifice of holding off his proposal, at this time, would have it's reward in the end. If she didn't hear from Victoria by the end of the summer, he could always propose to her then. With a gentle good night they parted ways.

Back in her apartment, Katelyn stood by her window looking at the clouds that lazily floated over the moon. It was a beautiful sight to see the moon beams streaking through the small gaps in the clouds. It had been an awesome night with Rolland in the park, especially since they had nearly lost themselves in each others embrace.

As she stood dreaming about the events of that evening, Katelyn put together a poem that surfaced from deep within the recesses of her mind.

Fires of Passion

He beckons me with his eyes,
    and the way of his speech.
Causing a spark of desire
    to burn deep within me.

I want to reach out and embrace him
    tightly in my arms.
To passionately caress his lips
    with my own.

It is a fire of passion that burns
    deep inside of me.

All night long, my mind is tormented
    by desire to be near him.
While my heart throbs,
    and my body trembles,
        my mind races on.

It is a unique thing------------,
    the imagination.

> I feel his presence,
> as though he was near.
> My body cries in anguish,
> "Reach out and touch him,"
>
> But alas--------------
> he is not here.
>
> Shall I cry out,
> to relieve my thoughts?
> No! No! Oh the bliss.
>
> The night moves on----------,
> my imagination grows.

Katelyn got some paper from a drawer in the kitchen and then sat down by the table to write out the poem that had come to her. She was normally not into writing poetry, although she had written two or three in the past, but this one had come to her so clearly that she had to write it down before it left her for good. There were a few times that she had put poems together in her mind, but never written them out, and they were gone forever.

Throughout the night, Katelyn dreamed again of Rolland coming to her and carrying her away with him. There were three or four dreams like that, none of them the same, but never once did he propose to her. Her heart yearned in each dream for him to ask her and all that happened was that he would take her away with him. She did not know where they went, because none of the dreams revealed to her what would take place after they were gone. Each dream had come to an abrupt stop at that point, but in each dream she had been filled with anticipation, while her nipples stood out in ecstasy. Her heart throbbed and her hormones ragged in her body.

Suddenly, Katelyn bolted upright in her bed in a cold sweat. Her nightie was damp, cold, and clammy as it stuck to her skin. Although it was a warm night in late May, she shivered as she got out of bed. From her dresser, Katelyn pulled a warm flannel night gown. She quickly slipped out of the nightie and put on the flannel gown. Immediately she began to feel the warmth coming into her body.

Walking over to the window, she looked out into the night. It was barely two o'clock in the morning according to the clock on her night stand. As she looked into the night, Katelyn pondered over the dreams she had. What did they mean, and why did they all stop abruptly when Rolland took her away. Where did he take her? It didn't really matter, they were just dreams, but Katelyn once again wondered if they meant anything.

"Well Rose," she said out loud, "At least you got to find out what it was like to be intimate with Jack. I might never know what it will be like with Rolland."

Getting back into bed, Katelyn lay awake for a long time thinking about Rolland. She smiled as she thought back at what had happened at the fire pit. How foolish she had felt when they fell off the bench. It was a good thing that nobody had been around to see it. 'Nobody had been around.' The thought hit her like a ton of bricks. That was it! In order for them to keep the vow they had made to each other, to abstain from sex outside of marriage, the thing to do was to make sure that there was always other people close by. They had started being together with others present, and had not come to Indian Battle Park in the late evenings, for just over a month. Katelyn had been so excited to have Rolland back that she forgot they were not going to be alone in the Park late at night. She must never let herself forget that again no matter how her hormones acted because she missed Rolland. Her love and desire for him was growing stronger with each passing day.

With this thought in mind, Katelyn drifted off into a peaceful undisturbed sleep.

CHAPTER ELEVEN

FOR TWO WEEKS ROLLAND was very busy with clients so Katelyn only saw him periodically, mostly they would have coffee on Fridays after Katelyn was done work. Rolland needed his sleep with the work load he had on him, so Katelyn didn't pressure him to see her more often. On one of her days off, she went to Head Smashed In Buffalo Jump near Fort Macleod, only about forty five minutes west of Lethbridge. She wanted to know more about how the Blackfoot would run the buffalo over the cliff to get their winter supply of meat. It was an exciting couple hours she spent looking at the exhibits and watching the short film they had in the theater. Katelyn was excited on her way back home. She had managed to follow a touring group, while she was at the center and heard the guide tell many interesting stories about the

Jump itself, and also about Napi the trickster god of the Blackfoot people.

Katelyn stopped along the roadside on the way back to Fort Macleod to take a couple pictures of a split rock the guide had talked about in a story about Napi the trickster. She had much to think and dream about with this visit to the Buffalo Jump. At Fort Macleod she stopped for coffee and some fries before proceeding on home. Her mind was just buzzing as she drove the thirty minute drive to Lethbridge. What an experience it must have been to see all those buffalo run over the cliff to their death. Then all the work it took to prepare the meat for drying so it could be used during the cold winter month for food supply, along with the berries they would find along the river side. Tools and utensils were made from the bones and horns. The hides were prepared and cured for use in bedding and clothing, along with material used for the building of new tepees. It was interesting how they had used dogs in harnesses to help move things before the horse came into their possession. Katelyn thought that the Blackfoot, along with all the natives of America, had been better off before the greedy white man came to take over the land. The native were satisfied with hunting for food and making their own tools and clothing, whereas the white man with all his greed wanted more and more, not caring about his fellow man. The white man had forced the native to conform to the white man's way, forbidding the native to practice their ceremonies and rituals. The white man had introduced alcohol to the natives, brought his diseases upon them, and treated them with disrespect. A tear rolled down Katelyn's cheek as she thought about how the natives had been treated. It made her ashamed to even consider herself a white man.

At home, Katelyn took out the pamphlets she had obtained at the Jump. There was so much information about the Jump that Katelyn lost herself in the material. She almost didn't hear the phone ringing as her mind was wrapped around the intriguing information of the Blackfoot life and activities.

"Hello," she answered the phone, her mind in a haze.

"Sweetie. Did I catch you sleeping?" Rolland's voice came over the receiver."

"Oh! No!" Katelyn laughed. "You just caught me in one of my dream modes.

"I understand Sweetie," Rolland assured her. "I'm phoning to let you know they are sending me back to Victoria to meet two new clients that are interested in us through the other client over there."

"That's good to hear Honey," Katelyn replied.

"But I will be gone for at least one week," Rolland added.

"I understand how important your job is," Katelyn breathed lovingly. "You support my dreams and desires, so the least I can do is back you up in your carrier."

"I feel so bad because I've been busy for the past two weeks, and now I will be gone for a whole week."

"Rolland my Darling," Katelyn laughed heartily, "Absence makes the heart grow fonder."

"I love you so much Katelyn, and even though we only went out for coffee a couple times the past two weeks, my heart melts when I think of you during the day. I want you to know that there are times every day that I literally have to stop my accounting and bring my mind back to bare on my work. It hurts not to see you, and now I will be gone for a whole week."

"Honey! It is also difficult on me that we are not together very often, but my love for you grows with each passing day. There are advantages to dreaming, but that does not mean it is easy being separated from you for such a long time. I understand what your job involves, and it excites me to know that they are sending you, instead of one of the other accountants, to Victoria. At least one of us is doing what they really desire to do. I so desire and hope to hear from Victoria that I'm accepted to work at their museum."

"I'm sorry you haven't heard by now," Rolland encouraged her. "I know how deeply you desire to get that job. I want you to know, I'm behind you all the way."

Katelyn smiled to herself as she thought, Propose to me you fool, and I'll forget that dream in my life. I have a greater desire to be your wife than I do to work in Victoria.

"I'll be alright, Honey. You just go do your job and make the company proud, because I'm proud of the work you do for them. I have my dreams to keep me occupied till you come back."

Rolland laughed, "Sweetie, your dreams keep you going whether I'm gone or when I'm with you, but my love for you also grows with each passing day and I want to be there to support your dream. I'm leaving early in the morning so I need to get to bed.

"Okay Honey," Katelyn sighed, "You sleep well and I'll see you when you get back."

"I'll call you every day to touch base with you," Rolland promised before hanging up.

As the phone clicked in her ear, Katelyn couldn't help feeling a bit down. She understood the importance of Rolland's job and that by going to Victoria and the clientele growing over there, Rolland would be coming to Victoria often. She knew how the company admired Rolland's work, and how they always picked him over any of the other accountants to go to outside clients. You didn't get where Rolland was by being slack in your job, but that didn't make it any easier to take whenever he left. What would happen if she wasn't accepted in Victoria? The thought of not going to Victoria jolted Katelyn momentarily, but she quickly put that thought aside. She would try to keep her thoughts on happy events.

For the next week, Katelyn packed a lunch and went to Indian Battle Park to dream, before her shift started at three in the afternoon. She liked her shift, because she was done at eleven and had plenty of time to get home before midnight and to bed. That way she had from at least nine each day till work time to study and dream.

As she arrived at the park, she always picked a certain Poplar tree and let her dreams take her away to whatever may come. She always set the alarm on her cell phone so that if she got too deep into her dream world, she could come back to reality, at the sound of the alarm, before it was time to work.

Laying in the shade of the cottonwood, on the morning of Rolland's departure, Katelyn had a twinge of heartbreak, knowing that he was leaving for a week. At first it was difficult to put her mind at rest to think of history, but she finally manage to succeed in calming her emotions and let her mind kick into dream world mode. As her eyes closed she saw the counsel fire and only two men sat around it. At closer glance, she saw that it was Many Scars and Chief Red Crow talking seriously.

"I have asked you to meet me here at this fire because I have a quest that I want your permission to fulfill." Many Scars requested of Red Crow.

"What is this quest you speak of?" Red Crow questioned. "You are a Shaman and if you desire to go and be alone with the Great Spirit to meditate then so be it. I trust your decisions and judgements more than anyone else because of the wisdom you walk in."

"It is not that, Great Chief." Many Scars made eye contact with Red Crow. "I desire to take my daughter Pretty Bird on a quest with me. I want to teach her the ways of the old ones before us. The white man has come into our midst with his fire water and diseases, and now the white man has sent a troop of mounted police to keep peace among the whites and natives. My quest includes taking Pretty Bird to the sacred place where those before us have put their writings upon the walls of the Hoodoos. It is my hope that Pretty Bird will desire a vision quest while we are at the sacred place of writings."

"You are a man who is wise beyond that of anyone I have ever known. You have traveled far in your younger days to obtain more wisdom of this world we live in, as well as to become closer entwined in your knowledge of the spirit world. You have far succeeded in all wisdom and I trust you more than I have trusted any mans decision. Your medicine is strong, Many Scars, so go take Pretty Bird and teach her what you know in your heart to be the right thing." Red Crow encouraged. "Help her to distinguish between the Great Spirit and evil spirits."

Many Scars left the counsel fire satisfied that he had Chief Red Crows blessing on his quest. Now he would have to convince Gentle Woman that this was the right thing to do. He had prayed many prayers seeking guidance from the Great Spirit, and all he ever sensed was that it was the right thing to do, and that now was the right time to do it. Pretty Bird was now nineteen summers old and many of her friends that age were already married some of them having a child or children of their own. Many Scars knew of Pretty Birds desire to marry Running Wild, and he had not yet chosen a wife for himself. Most young girls had given up to be noticed by Running Wild, but not Pretty Bird. Maybe they were meant for each other, but not yet. Many Scars believed that Pretty Bird would get married, but that she would be like her mother, not until she was at least twenty-one or twenty-two summers old. The past three summers as Pretty Bird grew older, she had come to her father for much advice. She knew that in his younger years, Many Scars had traveled far from home to gain wisdom. He had conversed with many Shaman from other tribes to learn their wisdom. He had also learned much about the white man and the Spaniards in his travels. Many Scars had promised Pretty Bird that someday he would pass this knowledge on to her. He felt in his heart that this was the appointed time to take his daughter aside and to teach her the true ways of the Blackfoot.

Upon entering their tepee, Many Scars addressed Gentle Woman. "I have thought hard and prayed often about this matter." He hesitated.

"Speak my husband," Gentle Woman encouraged him.

"It is a hard thing I must say," Many Scars met Gentle Womans eyes.

"My dear husband," she smiled at him. "You have always had a very soft heart but you are a great man of wisdom. No other such Shaman has ever been the medicine man in the Blackfoot tribe, or any other tribe if I may say so."

"You have always been an understanding woman, and a good wife. You have given me a daughter who is very dear to my heart. Now it is time to take our daughter on a quest that has been on my heart for many moons now. I want to take her away for a while to teach her the true ways of the Blackfoot people." Many Scars looked down at the ground for fear of what Gentle Woman might say to his request.

"You are a man of great wisdom, Many Scars," Gentle Woman spoke sternly, "But I do believe you have finally stepped into something that has not been done before. I have been unable to bare you a son who you could take and train, but our daughter is not a warrior. Girls are not trained in the same way as young men are trained."

"I know Gentle Woman," Many Scars swallowed hard to get rid of the lump in his throat. He knew it could be hard to convince his wife to let their daughter go with him on this quest, but it must be done. After all, he, Many Scars was the Shaman and he was close to the spirit world to hear from the Great Spirit. "I have prayed and sought wisdom from the Great Spirit, and this is what must be done."

"My dear husband," Gentle Woman took his face in her hands and lifted it up to look at her. "I have always trusted you to make the right decisions, and could I even now doubt the wisdom you have deep within you. Take our daughter and teach her well. I might not like it, but how could I ever stand in the way of the Great Spirit to have you do anything against His desire for our daughter's life."

Many Scars stood in awe as he heard what Gentle Woman had said. His prayer to the Great Spirit, after he had been instructed to teach his daughter the ways of the Blackfoot, had been, 'Help Gentle Woman to understand.' All these past three moons he had fretted for nothing. Even at his age he was still learning to lean and trust fully in the ways of the Great Spirit.

Noticing the look of surprise on Many Scars face, Gentle Woman came and hugged him. "My dear husband. I know that you are a great man and that with all your wisdom I must let go of my own desires and trust that you will always make the right decisions. When it comes to our daughter, it is harder to let go. She is so fragile and her desire to marry has caused her great pain. I hope she will be as willing to go with you as I was to let her go. I know she adores you and has great respect for your walk of faith"

Many Scars kissed his wife lovingly. "You have always been a good woman to me Gentle Woman. You have also always understood me maybe even better than I have understood myself. My desire to serve the Great Spirit is stronger than any other desire in my life. It was the Great Spirit that impressed upon me to take our daughter on this quest to teach her how to follow the right path."

As he was about to leave the tepee, Pretty Bird came inside. Many Scars smiled at her and gently asked her to sit down. After she sat herself down and made herself comfortable Many Scars spoke. "My dear daughter. It has come to me to take you on a quest to teach you all the ways of the Blackfoot. The Great Spirit has spoken."

Pretty Bird looked at her father and smiled at him before she spoke. "Father, I know you are a man who is very close to the Great Spirit. I have watched you in every area of your life. It has been my desire to grow up to be like you. In order to learn to be like you, I must be willing to make sacrifices and spend time alone with you. I desire to get married, but as you know most girls my age are already married and have families of their own. Maybe I can not get married. One thing you have taught me that has always stuck with me is that I must trust the Great Spirit to lead me down life's pathway. I'll go where ever you feel we must go to teach me the ways of truth."

Many Scars stood with his mouth open not being able to speak for a moment. He had thought that both his wife and daughter would put up such fight about her going with him on this quest. Truly this was a sign from the Great Spirit that his prayers had been answered. His heart melted as tears of joy poured down his cheeks. His love and adoration for the Great Spirit increased and he never ceased to be amazed at the awe and wonderment of His power. This incident even brought him closer to the Great Spirit than before.

Wiping his eyes dry, Many Scars instructed Pretty Bird, "I don't know how long we will be gone, but we better pack for a long journey, and many days, because I don't know where the Great Spirit will lead us in this quest, or how long it will take. I do know that I've been instructed to take you to the place where there are writings on the cliffs."

Katelyn bolted upright from her dream. Pretty Bird was going on a journey with her father. Did that mean that she might not get married? If that was the case, was that how Katelyn would end up as well. Maybe she wasn't meant to be married, and that Rolland and her were just to be friends for ever, but then they shouldn't even kiss each other. It was time to eat her lunch, but the thought of not marrying Rolland startled her. She had a hard time eating her sandwich, as every bite seemed to lodge itself in her throat. With a struggling effort, Katelyn managed to eat it one small bite at a time with water to wash it down. When her lunch was finally done, she couldn't help but feel a bit upset that she might not marry Rolland. Then she scolded herself for these feelings. After all, wasn't Pretty Bird and Running Wild her dream. Her mind would not allow her to go back to dreaming after lunch. The turmoil in her brain wouldn't let go of the thought that possibly Rolland wouldn't marry her. What was she doing with him then. She was not going to have sex with Rolland just to say she did it.

"Sorry Rose," she murmured out load, "I love Rolland, but I can't give myself to him if he is not going to be mine the rest of my life."

All that evening she was unable to shake the thoughts she had earlier that day. Although it left her a bit moody, she was still pleasant with the few customers that showed up that evening. The phone rang, and it was Rolland. This would not be a good time for him to detect the disappointment she felt, so she tried hard to disguise her true feelings.

"Did you have a good day?" Rolland asked when she answered the phone.

How could she have had a good day when Rolland wasn't going to marry her. "It wasn't bad," she managed politely enough.

Rolland noticing a slight difference in her voice, responded, "Sweetie, is everything alright?"

Katelyn burst into tears. Not wanting Rolland to know the real reason for her tears, she just blurted out, "I miss you so much. You've been busy for the past two weeks, and now you are going to be gone for a whole week."

"I'm sorry Sweetie, but I'll make it up to you when I get back. We are all caught up at the office so it will just be back to normal again."

"I guess I'm just being a softy and I desire to be with you, Katelyn cried. "I'll be okay, now that I cried a bit. I realize how important your work is to you, and I'm just being selfish by wanting you all to myself."

"You'll be happy to know that I already met the two new clients today, and beginning tomorrow they want to start on the book work right away," Rolland spoke joyfully.

Katelyn had control of her emotions as she replied, "I'm happy that all is going well for you over there."

"The two new clients both said they wanted to pass the word on to other businesses about our great service," Rolland laughed heartily. "That means I can come out to see you that much more when you get your job here."

"Rolland!" Katelyn sighed, "I sure do love you. How could I ever imagine that I'd lose you by moving to Victoria."

"You could never lose me Sweetie," Rolland was puzzled at hearing her speak that way. "Did something happen today, or did I do something to make you feel like you were losing me."

"No Honey," Katelyn burst into a new array of tears, "I guess I'm just emotional today, knowing that you will be gone for a week. Maybe that is what is wrong, but I promise you I'll be better tomorrow."

"Okay Sweetie! I'll be talking to you tomorrow about this same time." Rolland assured her. "I love you."

"I love you too Honey, and I'm sorry for crying," Katelyn sniffled.

After they hung up the phone, Katelyn reached under the counter for some handy wipes to clean away the tears from her face. She didn't want Tracy to know that she had been crying. How silly that she let her emotions get the best of her. Rolland loved her, and he had his own reasons why he didn't ask her to marry him. After all, the more clients the company got in Victoria, the more often they would see each other. The thought came to her, maybe it was better this way, because they were getting too close and had nearly gone to far a couple times. Being separated might get Rolland to pop the question sooner. Katelyn smiled as she thought about Rolland proposing because he could no longer be apart from her.

The phone rang and Katelyn answered it. "Valley View, Katelyn speaking."

"Katelyn," came an exciting voice through the receiver, "This is Jill!"

"Jill!" Katelyn burst out. "How wonderful to hear from you."

"I've been very busy the past couple months with modeling," Jill replied. "Just today a scout from Hollywood came down and auditioned me. They want me to work in Hollywood with some of the mainline designers."

"Oh Jill," Katelyn burst into a new array of tears. "How wonderful to hear you say that."

"I owe it all to you my dear friend Katelyn."

"How do you figure that," Katelyn was surprised.

"It was you who was willing to go the extra mile to help me get back onto my feet."

Katelyn sniffled, "I'm sorry for crying, but it seems that is all I want to do today. Rolland is in Victoria for a week, and then you bring me this awesome news."

"Why is Rolland in Victoria?" Jill questioned. "I thought it was your dream to go there."

"It is still my dream, but Rolland is such a good accountant that he now has three clients in Victoria." Katelyn once again took a handy wipe to her face. This crying had to stop. "I'm sorry for crying, but your news is so exciting."

"Yes," Jill's excitement could not be hidden. "They are flying me out there next week. It will be an all expense paid trip to see how I feel about working in Hollywood. After spending a couple days there, if I like it, they will fly me back to Calgary to get my things packed. My first month rent will be paid by the company. I'm so pumped up about the whole thing."

"I can't tell you how over joyed I am to hear this good news," Katelyn whispered as she felt a new burst of tears coming forth.

"Well," Jill burst into happy laughter, I just needed to share the news with you. I'll keep you posted about how things are going."

"Thank you Jill for this bit of good news. I look forward to hearing about your progress in Hollywood."

As she hung up the phone, Tracy stepped through the door. Taking one look at Katelyn, she laughed as she said, "Let me guess. More unhappy disasters in the history books."

"Oh no!" Katelyn managed to smile, "Jill just called to let me know that she has been auditioned to work in Hollywood"

"Katelyn," Tracy burst out with excitement, "That is the best news ever. Now I understand the tears."

Katelyn didn't think it was necessary to tell Tracy about the earlier tears. So she just went about getting ready to end her shift. She would be happy to get home to bed. "Tomorrow will be a new day," she breathed quietly. Tracy had gone to the staff room to put away her coat and purse so she didn't hear what Katelyn had whispered.

The night passed without any rough dreams to wake her up. Feeling good Katelyn took a shower before having a bagel for breakfast. Packing another sandwich for lunch she drove back to Indian Battle Park to lay in the shade of her favorite Cottonwood tree. Soon she was back into Pretty Bird's world.

Many Scars had two horses ready for them to ride, plus one horse was to pull the travois with the Tepee and the fourth horse carried supplies for cooking and eating. It was going to take two days to ride out to the sacred grounds where the writing was on the cliffs, because Many Scars didn't want to wear out the horses, and he decided that this would be a good way to start with teaching his daughter the true Blackfoot ways.

"Keep your eyes open," Many Scars informed his daughter. "I want you to observe this land as it is. Soon this land will change and it will no longer be as we remember it."

"Why is that father," Pretty Bird questioned him.

"The white man is coming to this land, and like the Spaniards of the deep south, the white man is greedy. He does not care about the native ways. Everything must go his way. He is not happy with just enough, but he wants to hoard everything he can for himself. The native looks after his own people, while the white man only looks out for himself."

"That is horrible, father!"

"Yes my child, I have seen it in my travels as a young man." Many Scars continued. "You must listen well to the things I tell you and teach you. These are things you must pass onto your children and their children. The Blackfoot way must never be forgotten. I have never shared the whole story about my travels as a young warrior, because upon my return, I started to share and our people laughed at me. Nobody would take me serious. After all, what was I but just a wanderer. The Spaniards destroyed the Aztec Indians because they were greedy for gold. They also destroyed many writings of the Mayan because they said it was evil. The white man only thinks his way is right, and he is forcing the native to live like them.

"Father," Pretty Bird interrupted. "Where are these Aztec and Mayan people you talk about?"

"I will tell you in time my child. First I must start at the beginning of my journey," Many Scars was patient with her, for he knew that she would have more questions as time went by. It was his intent to start at the beginning and teach his daughter about the ways of all the tribes he had the privilege to learn from, but most of all that she never forget the ways of the Blackfoot. Many Scars knew from his travels abroad that the white man could not be stopped. They had moved across the land in the United States, and were slowly taking over their land south of the boarder as well. The Mounted Police had come to put a stop to the whiskey trade at the different forts like Fort Whoop Up. It still angered Many Scars that so many of their people were affected by the white mans fire water. His people needed to learn that they might not stop the white man from gaining possession of the land, but they could at least leave the white man's drink alone. In his heart, Many Scars already knew that many of their people would fall victim to that dreadful evil drink. His daughter must know the truth so that the truth would keep her free from the white man's evil greedy ways.

The North West Mounted Police had arrived in the area to help stop the white traders from giving whiskey to the natives. This of course would help, but yet Many Scars wanted his daughter to know what the true life of the Blackfoot was meant to be, even though things were rapidly changing around them.

Katelyn enjoyed the fact that the Mounties had come on the scene to stop the whiskey trading, although she knew from what she saw on a day to day bases the effect the trading had done to the natives. She paused her dream about Many Scars and Pretty Bird to interject a dream about the Mounties coming west.

Colonel James Farquarson Macleod had received his orders to march a troop of North West Mounted Police to the west to stop the American whiskey traders from destroying the natives with this dreaded drink that they themselves concocted with additives like soap and lye. As they headed west, they had no guide to lead them and they got lost en-rout to their destination. Arriving at Fort Benton, Colonel Macleod encountered a half breed, Jerry Potts, who was willing to guide the Mounties to the area where whiskey trading was being done at Fort Whoop Up. Potts was disgusted by the whiskey traders for what their fire water was doing to the native people. It angered him that the fire water was unbelievably cheap compared to the value of furs and buffalo hides. He was at a loss what to do, because he was a half breed, it was impossible to fight against the whiskey traders. Now that the Mounties were sent to stop the traders, Jerry Potts was more than happy to show them the way and to help stop these traders. Although he knew that the Americans would find new ways to smuggle their whiskey into the hands of the natives, Jerry Potts was going to do his best to help Colonel Macleod in getting rid of the whiskey traders.

Colonel Macleod welcomed Jerry Potts help and they were off to Fort Whoop Up. After the whiskey trade was stopped, the Fort was sold to Dave Akers who in turn rented part of the fort to the Mounted Police.

It saddened Katelyn that law and order had come too late to the land before the natives were hooked on the fire water. Although the forts were shut down, the Americans smuggled the fire water to the natives in return for pelts and hides. It kept the Mounted Police busy, but for years the whiskey still found it's way into the hands of the natives. Fighting broke out among the natives under the influence of the fire water and it was destroying the true culture of the Blackfoot. Many Scars was determined to get his daughter to hang on to the native culture and hoped through her the Blackfoot might learn to respect the ways of the old ones.

Katelyn ate her lunch and then decided to go to the museum to volunteer her time till she had to go to work. She needed a break from dreaming about Pretty Bird and being in the Museum would give her the time she needed to collect her thoughts. Of course, she looked forward to coming back to Indian Battle Park the next day. She had to admit, dreaming about Many Scars teaching Pretty Bird the ways of the Blackfoot, truly kept her mind off Rolland, most of the time. She was glad she had decided to do a study on other native tribes. It occupied her mind, and there was so much to learn.

Work went like any normal day would as a motel clerk. Katelyn didn't dream about Pretty Bird because she wanted to leave that for her special spot under the Old Cottonwood tree in the park. She was happy when Rolland called and chatted for a few minutes. It was good to hear his voice and to find out that everything was going ahead of schedule with his clients.

The next morning she was excited to study and learn more about the different tribes Many Scars would have visited. Packing her books and a lunch, Katelyn drove to Indian Battle Park and once more settled herself down under the Old Cottonwood tree. With her nose buried deep into the books she brought, Katelyn was soon back into her dream world. Gone for the moment was any thought of Rolland. She was intrigued by native history to the point where he was on the back burner till a later time. Traveling around in history, as a dreamer, had its advantages. Especially a dreamer like Katelyn. She would be totally oblivious to her surroundings, as her mind blocked them out till she returned from her dreaming.

CHAPTER TWELVE

AS THEY SET UP camp for the night, Many Scars had put together a fire before tending to the horses. He stripped off the gear from the pack horse as well as releasing the travious from the other horse, before taking them to the small lake to drink. Pretty Bird prepared a meal while her father looked after their horses to get them settled for the night. While they ate, Many Scars was quiet, he had many thoughts of the years he had traveled to learn more about other tribes as well as the coming of the white man and the Spaniards. He had learned through his travels that you could not beat the greedy white man. Their hearts were so deceived that even if they lost a thousand men in war, they would come back with ten thousand more. Although these thoughts angered him, Many Scars knew that his people must learn to live with the white man but to always remember their own cultural background. Many Scars had learned that the Great Spirit they served was also the same Great Spirit the white man served. The white man had just not learned to draw close to the Great Spirit as the natives had. Although, Many Scars had to admit, not all the Natives walked closely with the Great Spirit. Many of the Blackfoot people even went about doing their own thing rather than follow the leading of the Great Spirit.

The white man and Spaniards had Spiritual Leaders who they called Priests. They read from a book they called the Bible, and the same men taught what they believed that book was telling them. Many Scars had desired to know the Great Spirit and to hear what the Great Spirit was saying for the people to do. The white men that he had encountered in his travels did not have the desire to share with others, but rather they wanted to gather all for themselves. Many Scars could never picture the Great Spirit as being greedy. Yes, the natives had their battles against other tribes, but those battles were not over rights of the land they lived on. Nobody owned the land, they just resided on it until a stronger nation drove them off the land to live elsewhere. In his travels, when he was younger, Many Scars had seen places where there was evidence that the existing tribe had not been the first people who had lived there. The writings on stone spoke of other nations long before. Even the Blackfoot had buffalo and deer skins with special events drawn on them. The white man drove the natives off, only to say that they now owned the land. Many Scars did not hate the white man, he just wished they would know the truth so that the truth could set them free from their greed, and that all mankind could live together in peace.

After their meal was over, Many Scars began to tell Pretty Bird about his journey through the land as a young warrior learning the ways of a Shaman. "I knew from a very young age that I was to be a Shaman, but the desire to wander was in my blood. At that time I did not know what the Great Spirit was planning for me. As I followed the old Shaman around, I learned how he did things and also the importance of spending much time in meditation."

The desire to wander and experience the life of other nations had grown stronger as Many Scars grew older. To spend more time alone with the Great Spirit, Many Scars had wandered for days away from the tribe. His name at that time had been Wanderer. Even as a boy, he had spent very little time with the other children. He would wander off to be by himself, only to return in the evenings for meal time. His parents had been concerned about his behavior at first, but in time they began to realize that there must be a special call on his life. They noticed that he paid very close attention to the Shaman and his rituals. The Shaman, who's name was Walks Alone, had also noticed this special trait in Wanderer. He assured the parents that he to believed that Wanderer would become not only a Shaman, but a very different kind of Shaman. He would be one to wander from tribe to tribe learning the ways of other people. His wisdom would grow, and many people would put him down for the way he talked and thought. Wanderer, through discouragement, would become a strong warrior for a time, but the calling of the Great Spirit would continue to work on his spirit until he yielded to the Great Spirits calling.

During his time as a warrior, Wanderer received many wounds which evidently got him the name Many Scars. As he was suffering from a lance wound in his side, he was tended to by Gentle Woman, Pretty Bird's mother. It was this tender care that cased Many Scars to fall in love and take Gentle Woman as his wife. While he was in a coma for several days, Many Scars had a vision that he was meant to be a Shaman, not a warrior. In the vision he promised the Great Spirit that he would obey and be a servant to the Great Spirit. Upon recovery, Many Scars remembered the vision, and started his duties as Shaman. He had talked with Chief Black Bear and Walks Alone. Both agreed that Many Scars, with all his wisdom, would be right for that position since Walks Alone had little time left to live. The people stopped mocking him, and began to respect him for who he was. Many Scars should have been dead with all the wounds he had accumulated during his years at battle, yet the Great Spirit had spared him so they realized that Many Scars must have strong medicine. Although he never again attempted to share his experiences with his people. Many Scars hid these adventures in his heart and grew strong in his relationship with the Creator. He decided that he would share these hidden things in his heart with his children who would appreciate the life Many Scares had lived as a young warrior seeking the ways of the Creator in order to become a Shaman. Since there was only a daughter, Pretty Bird would have to learn the truths about Many Scar's travels That night the sky was clear and Pretty Bird lay awake watching the stars as they twinkled. Never before had her father told her of his life from the past. Her mother had told her a few things that she knew, like, that her father didn't talk about his experience from the past because of the mockings he had received many summers before. Pretty Bird had seen in her father that he was wise in all his ways, and how close he seemed to be to the Great Spirit. He had taken the task of Shaman very serious. Now she began to realize the seriousness of her father. Chief Red Crow relied upon her father for advise, and out of all the elders, Many Scars was the most respected, and not just because he was the Shaman. Many Scars had promised her that the next day they would reach the place of the writings, and there they would set up the tepee, after which time he would share with her his journey as a young man.

Although it was hard to sleep because she was excited, Pretty Bird listened to her father snore. She couldn't help but wonder if Running Wild was also awake thinking about her now that she was not around. Pretty Bird was more at peace now that her friends all had husbands, and that Running Wild was still available. Even though she was excited to be on this journey with her father, she still desired to be in the arms of the warrior she had loved all these years. What was he waiting for? All the other girls were married, and he couldn't become much greater as a warrior than he already was, so why had he not approached her about being his wife. Was she going to be without a husband all her life. "No! It can't be!" Pretty Bird shouted out loud.

With a start, Many Scars was awake. Dazed he asked, "What is it Pretty Bird? Are you having a bad dream?"

Pretty Bird felt foolish at her out burst, "I'm sorry father for waking you. I was just deep in thought. I'll be alright now."

"Was it something I shared, or were you thinking about Running Wild again," Many Scars inquired.

"Oh father," Pretty Bird burst into tears. "I can never hide anything from you. You are filled with so much wisdom and knowledge. Yes I was thinking that maybe Running Wild will not want me and that I will never make any man happy."

Getting up, Many Scars came to his daughter and wrapped his arms around her. "My dear daughter. I hope that after this short trip is over, you will put more trust in what the Great Spirit wants from you, than what you want yourself."

"I'm sorry father," Pretty Bird sniffled, "I know that I should take an example from you. I have watched you being guided by the Great Spirit, and things always work out for you."

"My dear Child," Many Scars laughed, "I carry the scars of disobedience all over my body. Had I not listened to the mocking of others, I would not have these scars today. We need to be willing to let others laugh at us, but we should never miss the calling on our life."

"I will try hard to please you my father," Pretty Bird assured him. "What you have shared so far about your travels, has sparked a greater desire to be like you. My fleshly desires still get in the way but I will do my best."

"It is not I you need to please," Many Scars scolded. "It is the Great Spirit who you must follow."

"Yes Father," Pretty Bird smiled.

"You will learn to rely more on the Creator, than your flesh will yeild to his will." Many Scars promised.

To change the subject Pretty Bird asked, "Did you meet many beautiful women in your days of travel, Father?"

"Yes my child," Many Scars chuckled, "But my mission was to learn the will of the Creator for my life. I desired that so deeply that even though a few women openly told me they desired to lay with me and make me a happy man, I refused them because such things are wrong in the eyes of the Great Spirit."

"Did you ever share that with mother?" Pretty Bird was curious.

"Yes my child, I told your mother about my travels and about the women I could have had." Many Scars smiled into the darkness. "I assured her that she was the only woman I could ever want."

"Thank you for sharing that with me Father."

"I desire for you to learn all the truth my child, and then to live by that truth."

Many Scars went back to his own blanket and as he lay down, he whispered, "My child, listen to my words. Hide them deep in your heart, and let the Great Spirit be your guide."

Soon Many Scars was once again snoring. "Running Wild," Pretty Bird whispered softly so as not to wake her father again. "If you don't take me as wife, then it will be your loss." With that she closed her eyes and slept soundly.

Katelyn sat up in alarm. What Pretty Bird had just said, hit her hard in the heart. Was this a sign that Rolland might never propose to her. Was his job so important to him that he wouldn't have time for a permanent relationship with her. Shaking her head, Katelyn scolded herself quietly. "How can I think this way? Running Wild hasn't even spent time with Pretty Bird. Rolland always spends as much time with me as he can. Stop thinking these thoughts."

It was time for lunch, so Katelyn ate at a park table, and after finishing she decided to drive to the library to study a bit more on the different life styles of the natives tribes in the 1800's. The afternoon went by very fast, so fast that Kaitlyn almost lost track of time. She closed the book she had been reading and decided to take that one and three others she found home with her, because they would be interesting to study.

Her shift went by quickly, as it usually did because of her dreaming, but she could hardly wait to get home to study more about the native life around 1844 to 1850. The white man was coming west and many wagon trains were attacked by hostile natives. This didn't stop the migration of whites to the west. Everyone wanted a piece of the land for farming or ranching and they were willing to risk their life to get it. Many natives were friendly towards the white settlers, but there were those who fought them off. The land didn't belong to the whites, but they kept driving the natives back and claiming the land for themselves. The native is not greedy by nature, so many of them could not understand why the whites thought they had the right to come and take land while killing of the native food source.

Katelyn didn't want to lay down the books, but she knew that she needed to sleep. In the morning she could take the books with her to her dream spot at Indian Battle Park. As she slept, she dreamt about the large Prairie Schooners crossing the land to seek new homes. There were days that they covered many miles, whereas other days due to difficulties they would stop while yet in sight of the camp from the day before. It was a hard grueling task and many members of the wagon train became temperamental and a few fights broke out before the wagon master could bring things to a calm understanding.

Before people joined a wagon train, they were warned about the dangers, as well as the hardships they would encounter. Even though they were informed that there would be those who would not make the trek and they would die, greed for land and gold strikes drove them on. Everyone believed it would be the other man or woman who might not make it. The west was built on the backs of others who endured the hardships along the way. Many unmarked graves line the trails that came from the east and headed for the west.

After Katelyn arrived at Indian Battle Park, she took her books and settled in for another day of dreaming. She opened one of the books and found that the Crow Natives didn't want to be friendly with the whites. Although they didn't go out to kill them, they raided many farms and ranches of their horses and cattle.

Many Scars and Pretty Bird had their morning meal and were on their way once more. All day they traveled till they arrived at a place filled with hoodoos. Pretty Bird was amazed at what she saw and her mouth dropped open in wonderment. They traveled a little farther until they came to the spot where she noticed markings on the walls in front of her. They were breathtaking to look at.

Many Scars pointed to a place near the river where they could set up the tepee. It was only a short distance from the writings, and yet close enough to feel as though the old ones appreciated their presence. After the tepee was in place, Many Scars built a fire, and while Pretty Bird prepared the evening meal, he looked after the horses. They had brought along enough rawhide that had been braided into rope to make a type of corral that would keep the horses from running away. There was plenty of grass, so Many Scars knew that if it was needed, he could move the makeshift coral to a different place. Driving stakes, that they had brought along, into the ground he proceeded to wrap the rawhide around each stake to tie into place for the corral.

After the meal was over, Many Scars talked more about his travels in his younger days. He had traveled many days before he came upon the Crow tribe. The Crows were a people who separated from the Hedatsa Tribe. Two Chiefs of equal power and nearly equal amounts of followers, couldn't agree with each other. One group left the Hedatsa tribe and became the Crow Tribe. The Crows and Blackfoot had warred against each other for many years, so Wanderer was not sure how he would be received. Holding up his pole with eagle feathers attached, he had ridden his horse towards the camp. The Crow Shaman and their chief came to greet him. They assured Wanderer that they would be at peace with him as long as he was in their camp, although they kept eyeing his horses. Wanderer related through sign language that he was trying to find out how other tribes were dealing with the white man coming into the country. They showed great hostility toward the white man, so Wanderer only stayed with them one night sleeping in the open air so he could keep his horses tied to his wrist while he slept. As he left the Crow camp the next morning, Wanderer couldn't help feeling that he might be followed, so he kept checking his back path. By the end of the day he was certain that if he had been followed, they had given up on him and went back home. He knew the Great Spirit was watching over him.

For the next couple suns Wanderer just kept traveling South until he met up with the Cheyenne tribe. They were a very friendly people, and when Wanderer talked to them about keeping peace with the white man, they were quick to agree. They had already been introduced to the French speaking whites and were willing to invite them in to share the land. They had met with two men who were scouting out some easy passage for the white man to come west. That had been about forty summers earlier. These two men were called Lewis and Clark. The Cheyenne had no problem with Lewis and Clark, and they strove to stay at peace with the whites. The Cheyenne Shaman talked long with Wanderer, through sign language, and shared a dream with him. In the dream he had seen one army of whites after another coming in to destroy all that the native stood for. It was the Shaman's hope that they could always maintain a good healthy relationship with the whites so that they would not lose any more lives due to wars with them. Wanderer promised he would stop on his return home, whenever that would be.

Wanderer stayed with the Cheyenne for seven suns before moving on. He could not pry himself lose from the wisdom of this Cheyenne Shaman. While he was there, he had no fear of his horses being taken, and the Shaman had insisted that he come share the tepee with his family. The Cheyenne Shaman was excited that Wanderer, at his young age, already maintained much wisdom and insight into the well being of the natives verses the white man. The Shaman was willing to share his Spiritual beliefs with Wanderer. He believed that the Great Spirit's desire was for all mankind to live in harmony together, but he assured Wanderer that there would still be many wars between the nations, because the young warriors were full of fire and not ready to settle down. Meanwhile, the white man and Spaniard were still out to conquer the natives and drive them back. It had been very hard to leave the Cheyenne nation, but Wanderer knew he had to see many more tribes and nations before his journey was over. "You are my brother," the Cheyenne Shaman had insisted as he clasped his hand on Wanderer's forearm. Mounting his horse, Wanderer had felt a lump forming in his throat. Truly he had found not only a new friend, but also a fellow Shaman who he could also call brother.

He did not have to travel many suns before he was in contact with the Arapaho Nation. Although the Arapaho were enemies with the Shoshone, Ute and Pawnee, they had made peace with the Sioux, Kiowa, and the

Comanche. Wanderer was guaranteed safe passage as he traveled through the Kiowa and Comanche territory. The Kiowa and Comanche had already made a treaty with the white man many summers before. As he traveled these territories, Wanderer was welcomed with open arms by these three nations. Except for a few young bucks in each tribe, Wanderer found that these tribes as well wanted to live in peace. Years of fighting the whites and losing many braves, the natives were beginning to realize the futility of fighting any longer. The buffalo herds had dwindled as each nation got more and more horses which needed the grass lands to graze on. It didn't help that the whites were just shooting the buffalo for their hides.

When he arrived in the Ute territory, Wanderer was welcomed by the chief and after explaining what he was doing, the chief introduced Wanderer to their own Shaman. Through much sign language, the two Shaman understood each other. Wanderer had great respect for the Ute Shaman, because he was an elderly man with much experience. They spent much time traveling the country as the Ute showed Wanderer some of the many cliff dwelling places that had been occupied by other nations before their time. The two men spent a couple nights sleeping in the old cliff dwellings. It felt good just to spend time in these cliff dwellings along with the spirits of the old ones, as well as reaping wisdom from the old Ute Shaman. Wander wanted to gain as much knowledge as he could from each tribe he visited. Food was less important to him than to seek the counsel of great men who had gained wisdom by their dedication to the Creator.

The Ute Shaman shared that he believed that drought for many summers had forced these nations to move onward. Nobody knew who these people were, but they were a nation of farmers, because there were signs that the ground had been tilled and things had been planted in that area long ago. The things that were grown might have been beans, squash, and corn. The Ute's lived off the land depending upon buffalo, deer, bear, rabbits, and quail for meat. They also picked berries and pine nuts for grinding up to make a similar Pemican as the Blackfoot made. They were also finding it more difficult to find meat for supplies as the white man continued to move in on them.

Wanderer didn't travel far for about two suns, because he wanted to spend time alone with the Great Spirit. After leaving the Ute's while fasting for the two suns, Wanderer had a vision that after he came back to his own homeland, many of his own people would not listen to him at first. He would go through a time in which he would be a warrior and get wounded many times, but the Great Spirit would continue to work in him and make him strong among his people. His name would change, but he would not know the new name till the appointed time. He would have to travel on because there were tribes he must see who were not serving the Great Spirit, but rather the deceiver. He would also experience disappointments as there were still those who thought they could fight the white forces.

When the vision was over, Wanderer packed up and continued south. He came to the Navaho tribe. They were a very friendly people who raised sheep, which they had aquired from the Spaniards through trade. They also grew corn, beans, and squash as staple foods for survival. The Navaho were very crafted in making beautiful colored blankets. The Chief insisted that Wanderer take one of these blankets as a gift. The gift was accepted with great appreciation. The Navaho Shaman traveled around with Wanderer for a couple suns and once again he experienced cliff dwelling places. Some of them were of great magnitude. As it had been with the Ute Nation, the Navaho didn't build these dwellings. They had been built long before the Navaho came to that part of the country. The Navaho were already at peace with the white man, so Wanderer and their Shaman were in agreement together on that subject.

The time they spent together was a time that Wanderer learned more valuable lessons. The Navaho Shaman also felt that it was the Great Spirit's desire that all Nations live at peace with one another. He also shared with Wanderer that greed for riches and power would stop mankind from achieving peace. The white man would continue to believe they were superior to all other races in the world. This attitude and the greed for riches and power would eventually destroy the world. Wanderer bade the Navaho farewell, thanking the chief for the lovely blanket, and then proceeded on his journey toward the Apache Nations. As he approached the Apache nation he did so with caution because he had heard that they were a very aggressive fighting people, but he found that the Chiefs of the Chiricahua, Mescalero, and Lipan Apache Nations were in favor of being at peace with the whites. They had fought long hard battles against the white man but all in vain. The armies of the white man had kept coming with greater numbers each time, so it was time to surrender and live in peace with the white man. It was only the young Apache's that disagreed with the white man ruling them and putting them on reservations, so they raided many white man farms and ranches and stole their horses. The whites would fight back and when the army came, they could only find the peaceful Apaches because the raiders would vanish into the desert to await another time to raid again.

There was much unrest with these nations. Many of their warriors had vowed that they would always resist the white man, fight him, and try to drive him away. Wanderer was amazed at how many of the natives still couldn't understand that the white armies would continue to come in and slaughter the natives if they didn't succumb to the white mans demands. Although he didn't agree with the white mans greed, Wanderer knew no other way to survive unless the native got along with the whites. He also believed, as did the Navaho Shaman, that greed would someday destroy the white race. When Wanderer left the Apache, he was very heavy hearted with so much unrest among those nations.

For the next few moons, Wanderer met many tribes and nations under Spanish rule. The Spanish were very ruthless towards the natives. In search for gold, they slaughtered and nearly annihilated many tribes, as was the case with the Aztec Nation. When Wanderer came into the Aztec area, he was mystified by the great temples they had erected. An Aztec priest befriended Wanderer and together they traveled throughout the former Aztec domain as the priest explained how all was before the

Spaniards came and destroyed their nation, all for the sake of the greed for gold and silver.

The Aztec believed they were the chosen people, and their god Huitzilopochtli directed them to build a city in a place where he led them too. The city would be called Tenochtitlan, so in honor to their god, they had to sacrifice human beings to him. As Wanderer thought about these sacrifices, he began to doubt the Aztec served the Great Spirit. No where at any time in his travels had he ever heard any other tribe talking about human sacrifice to the Great Spirit. Because he wanted to learn about all nations, Wanderer did not judge his host about the things he shared. The Aztec had been greatly hated by other surrounding nations, but they began to build their great temples to honor their god Huitzilopochtli. These were the temples that still stood after the Aztec were nearly all annihilated by the Spaniard, Captain Cortez. Their Emperor, Montezuma, had presented Cortez with gifts of gold, and when the Spaniards saw this gold, they wanted to conquer the city.

The Spanish Catholic Priests felt it was their duty to destroy all artifacts of the Aztec because of their pagan beliefs. The Spaniards did not find the gold they so desired, and the remaining Aztec people were scattered abroad, but they still practiced their way of life and belief.

The Aztec had made what they call a calendar of time. The Whites and Spaniards also had calendars of time, but they shared the same type of calendar, which was different than the one from the Aztecs. According to these calendars, white and Spaniards, Wanderer learned what the Native called summers, were years, and the year he was now in, was 1846. What the native called moons of time, they called months and suns were called days. The Aztec had a calendar that was divided in two, but yet remained one large stone, as described by the priest. The stone had been large, but it had been lost due to the Spaniards building a new city over top of the ruins of Tenochtitlan. Wanderer shook his head in sadness, the whites and Spaniards knew nothing about the sacred lifestyles of others. Greed drove them to destroy everything they came in contact with, only to rebuild upon the works of others. It was not right for one nation to destroy what the ancestors of other nations had worked hard to build up. It was not the desire of the Great Spirit that man should destroy the earth with his foolish desires of greed.

The Aztec calendar had three hundred sixty five days just like the white and Spaniard calendar, which they called a year, but the Aztec also had a two hundred sixty day ritual cycle included in this calendar. According to the ritual part of the calendar, these were days in which different human sacrifices were made to their god. The Aztec believed that their god demanded that they tear out the heart of the human sacrifice and place the heart, still dripping with blood, on the alter for Huitzilopochtli. Although Wanderer was horrified by such behavior, he respected the priest for sharing this with him, and he was awed by the fact that the Aztec had been so educated in their ways. No other nation up to this point in his travels had ever erected great temples in honor to a god. All other nation desired to seek wisdom from the Great Spirit. Wanderer wondered if this was why the Great Spirit had allowed the Spaniards to come and destroy the great works of the mighty Aztec. True, the temples still stood as reminders that there had been a mighty nation, with awesome architectural minds, living in the area in times past.

A shiver came over Wanderer, starting from the top of his head to the souls of his feet. He felt as though the spirits from the dead sacrificed people were crying out for revenge. Was it possible that the Great Spirit was calling to him to let him know that the dead would be avenged, and in a sense had already been avenged when Cortez fought and destroyed the mighty Aztec nation. No man, Shaman, Priest, Chief, or otherwise had the right to take another human life and sacrifice it on an alter. Lives were taken during battles, but that was not the same as taking a life and burning the body on an alter. The Great Spirit had created mankind, whether it was Native, White, Spaniard or any other nation on earth, they were to be cared for in honor of the Great Creator. Wanderer understood that there were wars among nations, but these wars were due to the fact that mankind had not learned to live and share together.

The priest shared with Wanderer that he did not agree with his ancestors sacrificing human flesh upon the alters. He had learned from the Spaniards about the true God, and that the Great Spirit does not believe in human sacrifice, but rather a commitment from the heart to Him. Wanderer was warmed up inside when the priest shared that with him. He had felt deep in his heart that the Great Spirit was directing him on his journey as he sought truth. As a young Shaman in training, his only desire was to know the Great Spirit in a deeper way. He knew that this journey had to be taken in order for him to be of any use to the Great Spirit, as a spiritual leader of the Blackfoot nation.

As Katelyn came out of her dream land, she couldn't help wander if this dreaming was a sign to her that before she was ready to marry Rolland, she would have to go on a pilgrimage. Maybe it was Rolland that was being prepared for something bigger before they could ever think of marriage. The study of the Aztec had been an awesome experience as Katelyn reflected upon what she had studied while eating her lunch. It hurt to think of how the Spaniards had destroyed the very artifacts that the Aztec relied upon in their spiritual rituals. Even though they worshiped Pagan god's, that was no valid reason for destroying history in the making. There had been so much history, and now so many questions unanswered because some Catholic priests had decided these things must be destroyed. Katelyn could understand why they did it, but it still angered her to know that a nation had been destroyed because of greed for filthy lucre sake, as well as serving Pagan god's. Had they only spared the peoples lives, and showed them a different way, things would have been less complicated. Kaitlyn cringed at the thought of what the whites had done to other people of the earth. The blacks were enslaved, while the Chinese were treated like dogs as they hired on to build the railroad across the land. The natives were driven onto reservations so that the white man could gain more land to fulfil his own greed and lust.

Katelyn was angry with the white mans ways but she still enjoyed reading the history, so she decided to read about the Mayan Indians. She was glad that Rolland was away, not that she didn't prefer him to be with her, but she could never imagine him to be Cortez or any of the other explorers who destroyed such great nations as the Aztec, Inca, and Mayan cultures. Although this happened five or six hundred years before this present day, Katelyn couldn't help feeling sad as well as angry. Sad for the sake of these great nations, and angry at the way the Christians had tried to push their beliefs on these people by destroying what they had believed in for many centuries, and possibly many millennia. She agreed with Many Scars, if you have a better way, then show it by your actions.

The sun was hot, but it was comfortable lying in the shade so Katelyn put her book aside for the time being. She imagined, if that Old Cottonwood Poplar could talk, it would have many stories to tell. From the look of it, Katelyn estimated it to be over one hundred years old. It was so nice laying there, enjoying the warmth of the sun and the shade of the tree, that Katelyn decided a nap would be good. She drifted off to sleep, but only after setting the alarm on her cell phone.

CHAPTER THIRTEEN

KATELYN HAD GONE TO work after her nap in the Park. There was a convention in town so the motel was full for the weekend, with people arriving early to get a room before the Friday evening session. The shift went by fairly fast and when Rolland called, they barely had time to talk. Rolland let her know that he would be flying home Sunday. He had a few loose ends to tie up on Saturday, and since he was in Victoria anyway, he desired to visit the Butchart Gardens.

"I wish you were here with me Sweetie," he spoke earnestly.

"I wish that as well, Honey," Katelyn almost cried. "Enjoy your visit, and I will see you Sunday."

After coming home from work, Katelyn went straight to bed. She wanted an early start at the Park the next day, because she was excited to learn about the Mayan Indians and the great cities they had built.

The next morning she stopped to pick up coffee and a bagel before she headed for her favorite spot under the Cottonwood tree. When she settled down, she ate the bagel and drank her coffee before laying down to dream.

In the morning, when Pretty Bird woke up, her father was sitting around the fire cooking a fresh rabbit he shot with his bow and arrow. Although the Blackfoot used the white man rifles, Many Scars still liked the bow and arrow for small game. The roasting rabbit smelled good, but Pretty Bird knew from the dream she had that she could not eat. In her dream she had a vision of going on a quest in search of the truth. She had watched her father over the years becoming stronger as he trusted the Great Spirit for guidance.

"Father," Pretty Bird spoke softly, for she believed they were not only on sacred ground, but that this very ground was Holy, considering the dream she had. "I don't want to eat today."

Turning around, Many Scars looked at his daughter. "What is it my child? Do you not feel well?"

"I am fine Father," she continued to whisper.

Many Scars lowering his voice spoke with concern, "What is it my child? Why do you whisper?"

"I had a dream during the night, and I believe the Great Spirit is requesting that I fast and seek his desire for my life."

Many Scars was overjoyed at what he had heard come from the lips of his only child. Since the birth of Pretty Bird, he had believed the day would come that she would seek guidance from the Great Spirit. It had always been his prayer for her, and now she was ready for this quest.

"My daughter," tears welled up in Many Scar's eyes, and he had to swallow hard to get rid of the lump in his throat. "It pleases me to hear you say that."

"I have felt it in my heart for a long time, Father, but I had many mixed feelings as well. The desire to be with a man also stood in the way for me to obey."

"To obey is better than to go about our own way, my child."

"Yes Father. I understand. When you said that you had many opportunities to be with women in your travels, but refused because your deep desire to follow the leading of the Great Spirit, that was the deciding factor in my decision."

Pretty Bird hugged her father as tears of joy rolled down his cheeks. Her own eyes also glistened with tears. "I understood more after you told me the other night about how your quest for the Great Spirit outweighed the desire for a woman." She began to cry on Many Scars shoulder.

"My child," Many Scars sobbed with her, "Today you have made me a very happy man. You will fast, and in time, maybe two or three suns, you will have a vision of what is to be expected of you in your lifetime. I will fast and pray for you as long as it takes for the Great Spirit to reveal his truth to you."

"Thank you my Father," Pretty Bird dried her eyes. "It is a great comfort that you will fast with me since I've never done this before.

Many Scars pointed out the place where others had gone to be with the Great Spirit in solitude. It was a flat spot on top of one of the hoodoos. He would help her get up there, and for the next two or three suns, she would be without food. She would only have water to drink, and a buffalo rob to cover herself in case it got cold. He explained that in this time she would feel times of loneliness, and at times even desire to quit, but Many Scars assured her that the hardship she would face would strengthen her in the end.

Pretty Bird was nervous as they approached the spot where she would seek the Creator for guidance for her life. Many Scars helped her to the top, and once there, Pretty Bird realized that the only way back down was with the help of her father, unless she jumped down, risking broken limbs. She almost backed out of it as she saw her father ride away, leading her own horse back to the teepee. This was it then. She would have to stay until the Great Spirit was done with her. Her father had assured her that he would know the right time to come and get her down.

As the day grew hotter, Pretty Bird sat looking skyward. How long would it be before she heard any word from the Great Spirit. She looked over towards the Tepee and could see her father sitting around the fire. He was most likely praying to the Great Spirit to protect and guide his daughter. Oh how she loved and respected her father. He had faced many trials in his life, along with mockery from many of his own tribe members, yet he stood firm, until the people saw that his medicine truly was powerful. He had gained their confidence and had become the most wise of all councilmen.

The day went by rather slowly, and Pretty Bird was questioning what she was doing out here on top of this hoodoo alone. From time to time she looked over to the camp and her father was still sitting by the fire. He only moved when he needed to replenish the fire with more wood. She wandered how he could do this as often as he did, but then she had never experienced anything like this before. Possibly the experience brought such satisfaction that it was all worth it in the end.

"How could it not be worth it in the end," Pretty Bird scolded herself for having such thoughts. After all, this was a time to be spent communing with the Great Spirit. She knew that she must not speak out loud because she had to calm her own spirit in order to hear the Creator speaking to her. To sing or hum in a soft voice was allowed. That showed reverence to the Great Spirit.

The screech of a hawk caused her to look skyward. Carried by the wind currants, the hawk circled slowly over head. Was he there for Pretty Bird, or was he searching for food? As she watched the hawk drifting along, Pretty Bird thought about the wonderful creation that the Great Spirit had put together. Her people had a great life living off the land, and yet the white man was coming in with different ideas. Yes, they brought warm blankets, cooking pots, plus many other things made of metal, that were useful to her people. The problem was, they also brought with them the fire water that cause her people to do strange things, and then there were all those dreaded diseases that had killed many of her people. The white man should never have come to this land.

As the day grew hotter, a bee buzzed around Pretty Bird before continuing on her route to find nectar with which to make honey. A Meadow Lark called forth it's cheerful note for a while, and Pretty Bird couldn't help admire the sound he made. All of nature seemed to speak to her and cheer her on in the quest to seek out what the Great Spirit wanted from her in this life. Hunger set in before evening had arrived, but as she looked over to camp, she could see that her father was still sitting by the fire. Whenever she had glanced his way, he seemed to have never moved, except to bring more wood for the fire. It looked as though he wasn't eating either, but then he had promised to fast with her. Was he doing that in support of Pretty Bird, or had he planned that all along on this trip? Maybe the Great Spirit had spoken to her father and told him to take Pretty Bird to this place because she needed to go on this vision quest.

As night came, the air felt a bit cooler so Pretty Bird wrapped herself up in the buffalo robe. Her thoughts went to her mother, and she hoped her mother was not worrying. She also let her mind drift off to Running Wild. Why had he not taken a wife? More importantly, why had he never noticed Pretty Bird? Even though she had bound up his wounds and taken care of him after the battle with the Cree, he never acknowledged that he appreciated what she had done. Maybe he resented her for saving his life. If he had died in the early morning hour of that day, he would now be in the Happy Hunting Grounds.

"Stop thinking about Running Wild," Pretty Bird scolded herself out loud. "You have to concentrate on meditating on the vision the Great Spirit will show you."

The sound of a coyote howling, sent shivers down her spine. It was a lonely mournful howl, but Pretty Bird was happy that the coyote had brought her senses back to the purpose of this time out here on this hoodoo. "Thank you coyote," she breathed softly, "Your howling couldn't have come at a better time. I must not concentrate on my fleshly feelings and desires, but rather on the quest I have taken upon myself."

From her fathers camp she heard a drum beat, and then her fathers chanting voice drifted through the cool evening air. Although he was quite a distance from the hoodoo where she sat, Pretty Bird could see and hear her father. The coyote had ceased howling and her fathers chanting was like music to her ears. Silently she began chanting and it made her feel less lonely as she sat huddled with the buffalo robe around her shoulders. Soon she began to feel tired, so she laid down and with her fathers chanting still drifting out to her, she fell asleep.

As she slept, Pretty Bird dreamed that Running Wild was coming towards her as she stood outside the teepee. He had such a look of seriousness about him that Pretty Bird wasn't sure what to expect. Standing in front of her, his masculine body showing forth the strength that lay within, he looked at her for a long moment without speaking. Pretty Bird, her heart beating fast, and her breathing seeming to choke up in her throat, could only look longingly at the man she desired to spend her life with.

"Why have you refused to marry the braves that have sought you for a wife?" Running Wild spoke as though he was uncertain of what to say.

"I wasn't ready for them," is all she could manage to say.

"You helped to save my life three summers ago, and I have gone on to become a strong warrior." Running Wild was looking directly into her eyes. "I do not understand why you would risk your life to save mine. It has puzzled me the past three summers, and now I have decided to ask you for the reason."

Pretty Bird, waking from her sleep, took a moment to realize where she was. As she sat there for a while, she became angry within. How could Running Wild not understand that she saved his life because she loved him. Was he so filled with himself that he couldn't understand how others felt? She looked over to the place their teepee was. The fire was only red coals by now, but yet she could see the outline of her father sitting there. What was he doing? Why hadn't he gone inside the teepee, or even replenished the fire with fresh wood? Had he fallen asleep will chanting? Laying down once more, Pretty Bird couldn't help wondering if the dream had meant anything significant. Pretty Bird scolded herself for becoming angry in her dream. She was supposed to be seeking peace with the Great Spirit, not venting her anger towards Running Wild. Closing her eyes, she didn't notice the dark cloud build up towards the north, but she was soon fast asleep once more.

Her sleep was once more engulfed with a dream. This time Running Wild approached her as she stood in the meadow, watching her new pony nibbling at the fresh spring grass. Her heart melted within her as she saw Running Wild coming near her. She wanted to run to him and throw her arms around his neck and kiss him, but that would be very improper.

Standing before her, Running Wild never even cracked a smile. "Why did you save my life?" He demanded. I could have been in the Happy Hunting Grounds instead of fighting in this world.

Once more Pretty Bird sat up out of her sleep. She had not answered Running Wild before waking up. What was the meaning of these dreams? "Oh Great Spirit," she began to sob. "Show me what is planned for my life."

Laying back down, Pretty Bird noticed, this time, that the sky was no longer clear. Big black clouds had rolled in like waves on an angry sea. Her mind was tormented by the two dreams she had, and it angered her to think that Running Wild could be so disrespectful towards her after she had spared his life. It was a long time before she finally drifted back to sleep, but not before admonishing herself for getting angry again. The wind was picking up, and little spatters of rain fell, but Pretty Bird was snuggled comfortably under the heavy buffalo robe.

As the rain gently came down, Pretty Bird dreamt again. This time she was running in the meadow enjoying the wonderful warm sunshine after the long and cold winter. There were still signs of snow on the south slopes of the hillsides, but she didn't care. This was a great day to dance in the meadow, showing the Creator how she appreciated the sun and the warmth that came with it. As she turned and whirled about, she noticed someone riding towards her on a horse. Stopping her dance, she saw that it was Running Wild, and he didn't look very happy. The horse raced up to where Pretty Bird was standing and slid to a halt as Running Wild was already leaping off its back.

Glaring at Pretty Bird, he demanded, "Why did you come and save my life at the battle with the Cree?"

Pretty Bird stammered, as she was shocked by Running Wild's behavior. Never before had he even uttered one word to her. "That was three summers ago."

"Yes," he agreed. "And for the past three summers I have not been able to forget what you did."

Pretty Bird turned to leave. She didn't have to listen to this rude behavior, but Running Wild grabbed her arm, spinning her around to face him. The fury in his face said it all. He was angry because instead of riding in the Happy Hunting Ground, Pretty Bird had forced him to live here where things were coming apart with the white man showing up.

"You had no right to take happiness away from me," He screamed at her.

Pretty Bird didn't know how she could have mustered it, but from out of nowhere her hand shot up and slapped him across the mouth. Almost losing his balance, Running Wild staggered backwards and caught himself before he fell.

"Don't you ever touch me or speak to me again," she whispered to him.

Running Wild began to reply, but at just that moment a loud thunder crash startled Pretty Bird from her sleep. She sat up just in time to see a torrential cloud burst of rain. Pulling the buffalo robe over her head once more, she sat in total darkness pondering the meaning of these three dreams. Was the Great Spirit showing her that Running Wild was not to be her husband? Feeling the rain pelting hard against the robe, Pretty Bird just sat there most of the remaining night thinking about the quest she was on. Her stomach rumbled with hunger, but she had to ignore her physical wants, and concentrate on the things of the spirit. Somewhere in between the turmoil of her dreams, and the grumbling of her stomach, Pretty Bird drifted off to sleep while sitting up listening to the rain pelting the buffalo robe.

When sleep had passed from her, Pretty Bird threw off the robe, but it wasn't the warmth of the sun that greeted her. The sky was still overcast with heavy rain clouds, and the wind was blowing hard, threatening to destroy everything in its path. It did not promise to be a joyous day out here with no food to eat, and only her thoughts to keep her occupied.

"Stop thinking about food," Pretty Bird scolded herself out loud. "This is a time to concentrate on spiritual matters," she spoke to her mind.

Looking over towards the camp, she saw her father sitting by the blackened fire pit. She wondered if he had been sitting there all night, or if he at least had gone inside the teepee during the rain. He sat there, covered by a buffalo robe, as though all life had been taken from him. Momentarily Pretty Bird was startled by the thought that her father might be dead, but then her fathers voice came forth out of the recesses of her mind, "My child, remember this one thing while on your quest. Many distraction will come your way to cause you to desire to quit, but quit you must not. The deceiver will try any way possible to get you to stop your quest, but you must resist at any cost."

After hearing her fathers voice, Pretty Bird looked once more at the camp. Her father was no longer sitting there, and it startled her to think that it might have been a vision she saw the first time. "Thank you father for your words of wisdom," she breathed out quietly. She looked again at the teepee, and noticed her father coming out. He stood up and stretched and then looked towards the hoodoo where his daughter was on her quest. Pretty Bird wanted to wave at him, but she knew that it was forbidden to make any contact with others as long as the quest was taking place.

Although the day was gloomy, with periodical rain showers, and her stomach desiring food, Pretty Bird managed to make it through the second day. Pulling the buffalo robe over top of her head, she tried to keep herself busy with trying to decipher the dreams she had the night before. The last time when she had fallen asleep while sitting up, she had not dreamt at all. Was there something the Great Spirit was trying to show her. Her father had told her often, things would come in three's.

That night, the sky began to clear, and as Pretty Bird lay down to sleep, the stars began to appear through the breaks in the clouds. Pretty Bird smiled as she thought about how she had passed her second day of the quest. She had thought long and hard about her commitment to serve and obey the Creator. Even though she fought hard all day not to concentrate on her physical needs, she had stopped her thought process twice to relieve herself. Pretty Bird took only small amounts of water to prevent dehydration. Her father had already instructed her on fighting the desire to drink lots to over come the hunger, and her stomach wasn't even complaining that much anymore. During the night, she didn't have any disturbing dreams, only dreams of her in the meadow watching her horse chewing on the lush green grass. She was laying in the shade of an old Cottonwood Polar tree just relaxing. She knew her horse would not wonder far, and if she whistled it would come running to her. Since she had desired to be alone with the Great Spirit, her father had suggested she take this day and go away to meditate. There was much work for her to help with back at the teepee, but her father knew her desire to learn the ways of the Spirit, and that could only be accomplished by dedicated time alone meditating and fellowship with the Creator.

When she awoke the next day, the sun was already high in the sky. The dream from that night puzzled her, because she had never desired to spend time alone with the Great Spirit.

Her mind had only been on Running Wild. Looking over towards the teepee, she saw her father standing by the fire pit with his hands stretched upward. She had heard him mention before about getting alone and stretching your hands upward as a sign of total surrender to the Great Spirit.

"Great Spirit," Pretty Bird began to pray, in her mind, knowing that the Great Spirit could hear her thoughts. "Not too often have I prayed to you unless it was for selfish reasons. I see in my own father the dedication he has towards you. Although I am still young, I am willing to learn to submit myself to your will in my life."

Tears flooded her eyes as she looked up towards the sky, and without realizing it she lifted her hands up and stretched her arms as far as she could reach. Quietly she began to chant and as the moments passed by, her voice was lifted into a jubilant melody that lifted upwards as a sacrifice of her allegiance to the Creator. She fell to her knees and before she knew it, she was laying prostrate on the ground face down unable to move.

At this time, Katelyn decided it would be a good time to eat her lunch. She could continue her dream after nourishing her body first. While she ate her sandwich and drank a bottle of water, Katelyn thought about the dreams and visions the natives had when they went on their quests. It was interesting how these dreams and visions would speak of things to come and times in the future. She had heard and read about how some natives had seen dreams of the coming of the white man and how it was not possible to keep fighting them. History was such a great thing to study, and as it was in her case, live the excitement in dreams.

Katelyn was fascinated by the ways of the native people. It puzzled her why anybody would want them to change their ways. It was a simple life they lived, but yet they kept busy with daily routines of looking after the needs in the tribe. They suffered hardships due to wars and sometimes hunger from lack of food, but otherwise they all worked together for the purpose of supporting the tribe.

Many times the tribe would gather around a large fire to perform dances for rain, hunting expeditions, war, and such things. Each time the whole tribe would participate, wearing special clothing decorated with feathers, porcupine quills and the like. As the drummers beat the drums the people danced to the rhythm of each drum beat. Excitement filled the camp as the people chanted to the Great Spirit to hear their prayers and grant the tribe favor. These ceremonies had been passed down and practiced for many generations, and they were taken very serious.

CHAPTER FOURTEEN

IT WAS LATE IN the afternoon when Pretty Bird rose up from the ground. She had been in a trance for the better part of the day, because she noticed that the sun was already far down in the western sky. Looking towards the teepee, she did not see her father, but then his voice came to her from below, next to the Hoodoo.

"My child, is everything well with you?"

"Yes father," she replied. "I am ready to come down now, but how come you are here?"

"I received word from the Great Spirit that you were done your quest," Many Scars assured her as he reached up to help her down from the Hoodoo. "I also know that you have much to share with me."

They rode together in silence towards the teepee. There was a fire burning, and a couple small partridges were sizzling on a spit above the fire. After having her vision that day, it did not surprise Pretty Bird to find food cooking for her. Her father had also been communing with the Creator, and since he was already close to the Great Spirit in his walk, she could understand that the Great Spirit had revealed to her father that her quest was over. He had gone out and shot two partridges for them to share in celebration of the quest. When her vision was over, the Great Spirit had requested that she share this vision with her father. Normally people hid these visions inside their own soul, but since the Great Spirit wanted her to share with her father, then she would. After all, he was the Shaman for her tribe, so he was always in touch with the greater power.

After the meal was over, Pretty Bird told her father that she had been requested to tell him of her vision. "There will be a great migration of white men into this country. Although their ways are the ways of greed, lust, and selfish desires, we must not fight them. There are too many to conquer. The white man is self centered and believes he is a much superior race than any other race on the earth, but there are those among them who truly follow the ways of the Great Spirit. By destroying the ways and cultures of others, the white man will eventually destroy himself. Many of the whites are faithful to the Great Spirit, but in time the nation will no longer be allowed to worship the Creator openly. Just like they have tried, since reaching the shores of this part of the world, to wipe out the native way of worship, they will also stop all mankind from worshiping the Creator, except for those who worship false gods. In this way they will destroy themselves. Only those who worship the Great Spirit will be spared from the wrath to come. We will succumb to the white mans way of life, but only those who follow the teachings of the Great Spirit will make it in the end. The white man also has the truth about the Creator, but over time they have slowly begun to do their own thing, leaving love for others far behind. It was never the Creators desire for one nation to be greater than any other. All men were created equal, but as for the white man believing he is a superior race, it has caused him to lose sight of love for others. Not all natives know the will and ways of the Great Spirit. Only those who truly seek after the ways of the Creator will depart from this world into the world of eternal rest. All those who do their own thing will enter the world of eternal torment where there is no rest. The white man knows the way, but many have and will keep on falling away from the truth. Only those who seek the Creator with all their heart will truly be set free and live peaceful lives in this world. Although there will be many trials and wars the world over, only the true followers of the Creator will know peace in these adverse times."

Many Scars sat quietly listening to his daughter, and when she was done, he smiled at her. "My child," he spoke gently to Pretty Bird, "All these things you have shared with me have been locked up inside myself for these many summers, because others thought I was crazy when I came back from my travels and shared things with them. I too had a vision like the one you had, but because of what others thought of me before, I dreaded to share with them. Not even Red Crow, or his father before him, know about these dreams and visions."

"Father," Pretty Bird was astonished, "Why would our people not believe what you as the Shaman have to say."

"Not all of our people serve the Creator, my child," Many Scars face had grown somber. "As it was in my travels, I learned that not all tribes worship the same. We all have different rituals we perform, but the Great Spirit showed me in a vision, it is not the rituals that impress Him. He is impressed with what is in our hearts."

"I want you to know, Father," Pretty Bird reached over and touched his arm. "After this time spent with you, and the time spent on the quest for the Great Spirit, I no longer think of being Running Wild's wife. I was selfish in my thinking and my ways, and I know that was not how you taught me to live."

"My dear child," Many Scars hugged his daughter, "After this trip is over, you will be married, and bring me grandchildren that I can enjoy in my old age."

Pretty Bird laughed, "I will try my best father, but just so you know, having a man in my life is no longer number one. It is the Creator who I want to serve the rest of my days here in this world."

Katelyn sat up and stared off across the park. Pretty Bird didn't care anymore if she married Running Wild or not. Was that a sign for her to stop thinking so much about Rolland. How could she ever stop thinking about the man she desperately wanted to spend the rest of her life with. Of course, her relationship with Rolland was still different than that of Pretty Bird and Running Wild. Pretty Bird didn't know what it felt like to be in the arms of the man she desired to be with. Katelyn knew what Rolland's kisses did to her. Her heart fluttered whenever their lips met, and she would have to fight hard to get control of her deep desires to go all the way with him. How could Pretty Bird just suddenly give up on Running Wild. Of course, Katelyn didn't know what it felt like to spend time alone in a fast for three days. Could it be possible that your hearts desire could change after spending three days without food, and no communication with another human. Katelyn admitted, she didn't even know how to pray. She had never been brought up that way even though some of the kids at school had been so called religious. Her desire to abstain from sex before marriage had nothing to do with religious morals, she had just decided that her body was only for the man she married. If that meant that she would never marry, then she would just never experience sex. Maybe she was like Pretty Bird in that respect. She no longer thought about a man being important in her life, and Katelyn didn't care if she never experienced sex. When Rolland came back, she would just be more careful where she spent time alone with him.

When she arrived for work, Katelyn had mixed feelings about her dream that morning. It puzzled her that Pretty Bird could just shut off her desire to be with Running Wild. Rolland was not even close to here at present, and her heart yearned and ached for him. A tear trickled down her cheek. 'Why couldn't he just propose to her?' Katelyn knew her desired dream was to go to Victoria, but she would gladly forfeit that dream just to be with her lover the rest of her life. She could still dream about history, but the added bonus would be the rapturous bliss of being in Rolland's arms from here to eternity.

The evening went by quickly, and then Rolland's call came. "Oh Honey," Katelyn burst into tears. "I'm so happy to hear your voice."

"It's only one more day," Rolland assured her. "Things went better then we had figured they would, so I went to the Bouchard Gardens, like I told you I would. I also seen a couple other tourist attractions, but it would have been nicer if you had been there with me," he continued. "I will be home by lunch time tomorrow."

"I just miss you so," Katelyn sniffled.

"I miss you too, Sweetie," Rolland swallowed hard to get rid of the lump that suddenly formed in his throat. The thought of Katelyn distressed made it hard for him not to just ask her to marry him, but he knew that her dream was important to her. There was no way he was going to have his proposal, and her not fulfilling her dream, hanging over his head the rest of their life together. It was a small sacrifice to make with great benefits in the end. When the time came, Katelyn would understand the sacrifice he had made to get her to see her dream come true.

"Sweetie, I'll call you again tomorrow morning before boarding the plane." Rolland had to go before he broke down and cried as well.

"Okay Honey," Katelyn tried to sound reassuring.

After they hung up, Katelyn grabbed a tissue and dried her tears. She sighed as she reflected on her breaking down and crying over the phone. She had also detected the hesitation in Rolland's voice as he spoke. She knew that he too must have felt the need to shed a few tears. Her mind drifted back to the dream about Pretty Bird. Many Scars had said that now she was ready to accept a husband. Did that mean that she, Katelyn, had to see the results of her dream before she could get married. She snickered silently over the thought. After all, it was her dream about Pretty Bird. She could end it anyway she desired, but yet the thought remained, would Rolland hold off till she saw her dream come to pass. Was that what he was waiting for? What a silly man, he could have her right now and she would sacrifice her dream for his love. Rolland was far more important than her dream. Although Pretty Bird had willingly let go of Running Wild, and though she was now ready for marriage, did that mean another brave would take her to be his wife. A chill ran up and down Katelyn's spine. She could never give up on Rolland, the dream would be forfeited long before she ever gave up on him. What was wrong with Pretty Bird anyway? Katelyn had to admit, Pretty Bird had received fulfillment in her life, but she had to submit to the Great Spirits desires for her first.

"Okay, Great Spirit, Holy Spirt, Creator, or God. I don't know you, but I'm willing to ask you to help me through to the end," Katelyn blurted out into the air. "Give me the strength to endure to the end."

The evening passed by, and as Katelyn climbed into bed she had a feeling of peace surrounding her. Tomorrow would be a whole new day, and Rolland was coming home. She would strive to endure to the end, while her dream became the main thing she would concentrate on. Rolland would be there, or he wouldn't, but her life had to center around her dream.

As she lay down in her usual spot the next morning, Katelyn still felt at peace. Had her prayer, the night before, really made that much of a difference. Rolland had called to let her know he was just getting on the plane, but it would still be a couple hours before he arrived at home. Katelyn's heart melted at the thought of seeing her lover again. Closing her eyes, she saw Many Scars and Pretty Bird still sitting around the evening fire. It was still early, so the sun had not yet set, and Katelyn notice such a peace gravitating around Pretty Bird. The fast and vision quest for three days had seemed to change her.

"Father," she looked lovingly at Many Scars, "Do tell me about the great Mayan tribe."

"Well my child," Many Scars smiled at her. The Mayan's were a great tribe about fifteen hundred to two thousand summers ago."

"That was a long time ago father," Pretty Bird was shocked to hear about so many summers back.

Many Scars assured her that it was a long time ago, but the Mayan like all other tribes came from somewhere way back many summers before that. The Mayan had adapted themselves to live in the wet climate of the rain forest. They learned to raise crops that were suited for that area. Corn was the main crop grown, and was a staple food for them. They were a people of great knowledge and skills. They also, like the Aztec had created a type of calendar with three hundred and sixty five suns in it. These suns were called days, and all the days together made up one summer which was called a year. The year was split into what was called months. The days and months were what the white man and Spaniards had on their calendars, but the Mayan calendar was made up of the same type of things just a bit more complicated.

There are twelve months in the white and Spanish calendar year. Some months had thirty-days in it and some had thirty-one days. There was one month that had twenty-eight days in it. Each of these months added up made three hundred sixty-five days. Each year was numbered, and according to the calendar it was now the year 1846. Wanderer found out that he had been born 1824 and at age twenty in 1844, he had started his travels, in search of the truth about the Great Spirit.

Wanderer had met a Mayan priest, named Ac Yanto, who had learned much from the ways of the Spanish priests. He did not agree with human sacrifices, and agreed with Wanderer that they had a different god than the true God.

From Ac Yanto he found that there were eighteen months with twenty days each on the traditional Mayan calendar. That made only three hundred sixty days, but Ac Yanto explained that the remaining fives days were unlucky days, and although they were still used they were treated that way. They no longer followed the old calendar, but had adapted to the Spanish calendar, although some of the old ones still preferred their own traditional calendar. Ac Yanto was not young, but he had been schooled by the Spanish priests, so he no longer practiced the old Mayan way. The Mayan, like the Aztec, had built large pyramid shaped temples on which the human sacrifices had taken place. Ac Yanto desired to take Wanderer to see one of the sites close by. He explained it would take a couple days travel to reach the lost city of Tikal. Wanderer agreed that they should go see this long abandoned site. While they camped at night, Ac Yanto explained to Wanderer about the Pyramid Temples and palaces that were built for the rulers and priests to live in. He also explained that they had been abandoned over a thousand years before. The land, being wet most of the year, had been used for the same crop year after year and finally couldn't grow any more because of over use. The Mayan had also grown to be a mighty nation, and over population had caused incurable diseases to spread through the people until they had died off in multitudes. The Mayans left the beautiful cities and moved to a new area to form smaller groups, with each group having their own rulers. Rivals broke out among the tribes, and through wars many more were killed off.

When the Spaniards had arrived, their priests called the Mayans pagans with pagan gods, and they destroyed the artifacts that the Mayans held dear to their heart. The Mayan had developed a paper like substance made out of a crushed bark and lime stone paste. On these papers were written the history of the Mayan people. It was just like the white man and Spaniards Bible that Wanderer had seen with many pages of writing on them. There were many other books that they had with writings on the pages. Because the Mayans were wise in architectural ways, and their mathematical skills were phenomenal, Ac Yanto believed that the way to build the pyramid like temples and palaces, for the priests and rulers, must have been written on those sheets as well, along with the instructions of their daily spiritual rituals. All these things the Spaniard priests had demanded to be destroyed by fire. Although the Mayan had been introduced to the Spanish religion, many of them still secretly performed the rituals of their old ancestors. They no longer used humans to sacrifice, but they would use birds and animals instead.

Ac Yanto shared with Wanderer that there were too many lost cities for them to explore, but they would all be replicas of the one they were about to visit. It would take months, and possibly years to find all these lost cities.

Wanderer assured Ac Yanto that he would see enough with just this one city they were headed towards.

When they arrived at Tikal, Wanderer felt once again, as he had in the Aztec city, the cry of the long deceased spirits of the sacrificed dead. It was like they were crying out for the people to change their ways. "Oh Great Spirit," Wanderer sighed, "Avenge the souls that were slaughtered here so many summers ago."

Ac Yanto smiled as he heard Wanderer pray to the Great Spirit. "My dear friend," he spoke assuredly, "I believe those souls have been avenged. The diseases that destroyed thousands, and then the wars, after the people split into separate tribes, killed off numerous more. You cannot disobey God and then expect life to be blessed."

"You are right my dear Mayan brother," Wanderer smiled at him, "But my heart is heavy for the ways of all mankind. I do not believe the Creator meant for people to fight and kill each other off. The white man and the Spaniards are filled with greed and so they want to over power all the nations and destroy even the land because they have no respect for her."

"That is the truth," Ac Yanto reached out towards Wanderer. They clasped each others arms in agreement together, that they would be friends and brothers forever. "I do not believe it was necessary for the Spaniards to destroy all that was written down by the Mayans." Ac Yanto explained. "The future generation can only keep buried in their hearts the stories told by parents and grandparents. Eventually my friend and brother, these stories will be weakened by time and so much will be lost and never remembered again."

"I will teach my sons and daughters the way to travel through life." Wanderer promised himself that he would never let his children forget the ways of the Great Spirit.

As they wandered through the ruins, Ac Yanto explained the best he could how the people one thousand years earlier would have lived. The peasants would have lived in the surrounding area, and they would farm, raising corn for their food supply. Once or twice a year they would come to the city to partake of the sacrificial rituals that were performed on a regular basis by the priests. Wanderer couldn't help being amazed at the great thought that must have gone into putting such a city together. All the work that would have gone into molding each stone and block into place. Although the jungle had enclosed itself around the city over the years, and the courtyard was littered with growth, it was still a beautiful sight to see. In his mind he could picture the priests and rulers bustling about involved with their daily duties, while the builders labored steadily day in and day out placing one stone upon the other as each temple and palace grew.

As they paused to admire one of the temple buildings Ac Yanto smiled at his friend, as he realized the intensity with which Wanderer just wanted to serve the Great Creator. All this magnificence seemed to mean nothing to him outside the will of God. Man could build great wanders to satisfy their own desires, but Ac Yanto could sense in his own spirit that nothing of this magnitude meant anything to Wanderer because it had not been built to honor the Creator. Yes, his eyes showed the amazement of such ability to erect these great buildings, but in the end, it had only been done for the praise of unreal gods.

"I believe my friend," Ac Yanto patted Wanderer on the back, "You will become a great Shaman in your own nation. I see by your expression that these ruins don't meet with your approval. I shall never forget you, and will miss you greatly when you have departed to return home."

"You have taught me much my brother," Wanderer looked at Ac Yanto with respect. "You are wise in your teachings. Continue to live your life true to the Great Spirit, and you will be an example to your people. Although we cannot control the desires of others, we can let the light of truth shine through us. Not all mankind will live with the Creator in the after life, but not one person will miss standing before him to be judged."

"Although you are much younger in age than I am," Ac Yanto smiled at Wanderer, "Your wisdom exceeds your years."

"I have learned much in my travels these past two summers," Wanderer replied. "I believe all mankind is searching for the truth, but most of them are on the wrong path, and so they will never find truth unless they seek the right path."

When they left the Mayan ruins, Wanderer couldn't help feeling relief. Although these were great and mighty displays of what can be done once mankind puts their mind to it, he knew in his heart that such displays of greatness would only fill the builders with pride. Only the simple life could keep someone humble before the creator. Man was not created to take the life of another person and place the body of the dead on an alter to be burned as a sacrifice. Wanderer shuddered at the thought of the rituals that had taken place in the Mayan temples as they ripped out a beating heart from the person to be placed on the alter. The priest, as he held up the still beating heart, would chant and wail his ceremonial apprecetion to the god they served. In his mind, Wanderer could hear the screams of the person to be sacrificed, drowned out by the chants and shouts of the worshipers as in anticipation they worked their minds into a frenzy following the priests example.

As the Mayan ruins were left behind, Wanderer sighed with relief that his mind was once again becoming peaceful. It was as though the dead at the Mayan ruins were also crying out in revenge, as it had been at the Aztec ruins.

On his journey back to his own people, Wanderer revisited the nations where he had become not only a friend but also a brother to the Shaman of those tribes. He spent a few days with them sharing the great wisdom he had learned from his journey. All the Shaman he had befriended agreed that it was useless to fight the white man any longer. Treaties would have to be signed in order for all men to live peacefully with each other. In his travels, Wanderer had also learned that the white man didn't honor the treaties he drew up. There had been tribes who had been placed on reservations after the treaty was signed, and later, after gold was found on those reserves the whites would uproot these tribes, moving them onto new reservations. Wanderer couldn't find it in his heart to hate the white man for what they were doing. It just saddened him that the whites were as greedy as they were. Destruction was surely going to come their way.

Getting back home, Wanderer was excited to share his experience, but the young warriors would have nothing to do with Wanderer's suggestion about not fighting the whites any longer. The old men were not sure what to make of this young warrior who was filled with what seemed like fantasies. Out of sheer frustration, Wanderer stopped sharing but hid these things deep in his heart. He knew that the day would come when his people would see too late that he had spoken the truth.

It saddened Katelyn to read about the destruction of artifacts that could have been useful in understanding the ways of the Mayan, Aztec, and Inca people. She wondered if these three nations could have originated in Egypt. After all, the Egyptians also had majestic pyramids and temples in honor of their gods. Could it not be possible that a group of Egyptians had made their way to the Bearing Straight and crossed it when the two lands were still attached together.

From her studies of the natives, Katelyn had learned that they had originated in the European countries. Since the Mayan, Aztec, and Inca had similar traits as the Egyptians had, there was more than likely a group of

Egyptians that had also crossed the Bearing Straight and had ventured further south where the weather was more like that of Egypt.

Closing her books, Katelyn got up to go meet Rolland at the airport. She knew he had his car parked there, but she missed him so much that she just had to see him. Studying the native ways had definitely been a benefit for keeping her mind occupied, but now that Rolland was almost home, she so desired to be held in his arms.

Katelyn got to the airport in time to see Rolland's plane land. Her heart leapt with such desire of seeing him and feeling his arms around her that she thought it would burst. As Rolland came through the door into the lobby, Katelyn rushed to him and nearly knocked him off his feet as she threw her arms around him. Dropping his briefcase onto the floor, Rolland wrapped his arms around her and proceeded to kiss her.

Both of them were oblivious of their surroundings for the moment. They didn't care what others might be thinking, because they were deeply in love.

"Oh Rolland Honey," Katelyn released her hold on him, but gazed into his eyes, "A week without you is way too long." She burst into tears of joy at seeing him.

"I'm sorry I had to leave for so long," Rolland's eyes were damp with tears of his own. Oh how he desired to propose to Katelyn, but he could not for the fact that it might cost her the dream of her life. His own dream was moving ahead in leaps and bounds. It would not be fair if he was the cause of Katelyn not fulfilling her dream because of his desire to ravish her with his love and intimacy, by marrying her.

"Honey," Katelyn sniffled, "It is Sunday today and I have the evening off. Why don't we pack a picnic lunch and spend the afternoon in the Park together?

"Do you think it would be safe? Remember what happened that evening when I returned from Calgary," Rolland questioned.

"I'm sure there will be plenty of other people there, with their children," Katelyn responded, while drying her eyes.

"Okay Sweetie," Rolland smiled at her. "It will be wonderful to share with you the great week I had with the two new clients."

"Thank you, my Darling Rolland," Katelyn smiled back at him.

"First I must go home and change out of my suit," Rolland commented.

"If you go change," Katelyn replied, "I'll go to the grocery store to get something for the picnic and we could meet at Indian Battle Park under the old Cottonwood Polar you found me under upon returning from Calgary."

Rolland agreed and they left each other to get prepared for a wonderful afternoon together. It would be a challenging time, with both of them desirous for the other. Katelyns heart was racing as she got into her car. She hoped that there would be lots of people in the park or she might be tempted to overrule her vow.

As she drove to the grocery store, Katelyn began to think about the clients Rolland had in Victoria. There were three now, but the number could increase, and if that happened, the firm might move him to Victoria. What would happen if Rolland did move there and she didn't get the job at the museum? Would he propose before he left, so they could marry and be there together?

"Rolland, my Darling Rolland! How I desire to be your wife!" Katelyn began to sob as she pulled into the parking lot of the grocery store.

She sat in the car for a few minutes to get control of her emotions. Katelyn hoped again, that there would be lots of people at the Park, because she was afraid she might not be able to resist being intimate with Rollad at this point in time. Her nipples stiffened as her breasts rose and fell with her deep breathing, at the thought of being intimate with the man she so deeply loved.

"Okay" Katelyn sighed. "Cool your jets. This is not a good time to get emotional."

Katelyn sat in the car for a few minutes to let her body settle back down. Every fiber in her being seemed to scream at her, as her hormones ravaged her body in response to let herself go and experience what Rose experienced with Jack in the back of that car the night of the fatal disaster of the Titanic.

"No! I will not!" Katelyn yelled at herself.

A woman walking past her car, stopped as she heard Katelyn yell. Not understanding why someone, alone in a car, would yell, the woman shook her head and moved on.

Embarrassed at her outburst, Katelyn decided to shop at a different grocery store. She didn't want to run into anyone else who might have heard her yell. After getting the things they could eat at the picnic, Katelyn proceeded to drive to Indian Batle Park.

Rolland was not there yet, so Katelyn hauled all the stuff over to the Cottonwood. After buying the car, she had put a blanket in it, along with a few other emergency items, which Rolland had advised her to do. She was happy to see the park filled with parents and their children. Katelyn knew they would be safe even though her body still quivered with desire for her lover.

She laid the blanket out in the shade of the Old Cottonwood Poplar and then proceed to arrange the food on it. Her mind was so absorbed in the thought of desiring to be Rollands wife, that she never saw him pull up in the parking lot. It wasn't till he was approaching her that she happened to look up and see him. The sight of Rolland caused her heart to skip a beat while her sexual desires erupted like lava spewing forth from a volcano. She wanted to leap into Rollands arms and kiss him passionately, but fought off that desire for fear she wouldn't be able to stop herself.

"Wow! This looks good," Rolland praised Katelyn as he stood and admired what she had brought to the picnic.

"Thank you Honey," Katelyn choked down her emotions. "I want us to enjoy the afternoon together. You have been gone far too long."

"Being here with you is wonderful in itself, without all this food," Rolland laughed. "You don't have to spoil me to make life with you fulfilling."

"They say that the way to a man's heart is through his stomach," Katelyn grinned at him. "Today I will try my best not to go into dream mode."

"Sweetie," Rolland put his hands on her shoulders and looked deep into her eyes. "Dreaming is what makes you the person you are. I love you for who you are, and being with you as you dream, warms my heart. Besides, as you dream, we don't get into trouble by going to far.

"Honey," Katelyn brushed his lips with hers. Rolland wasn't aware of how intent her dreams became, especially when he was in them. "You are such a caring considerate man. I don't know what I would do without you."

Rolland looked admiringly at Katelyn, then kissing her, he replied. "I want to see you have your dream fulfilled. Since I fought hard to get where I am today, I want to fight hard to see your dream come true in your life."

Katelyn smiled as she thought, just propose to me and that part of my dream will be fulfilled. She kissed Rolland passionately and her whole body tingled with anticipation as her hormones suddenly kicked into overdrive. The man was going to have to propose to her soon before she couldn't handle her emotions any longer. As her body quivered with desire, she pushed away from Rolland and blurted out, "No!"

"What is it Sweetie," Rolland was shocked at the outburst, but he understood as he had felt her body quiver as they were pressed close together. Warning lights had gone on just before Katelyn had released her hold on him. Although he had not seen her for a week, Rolland had promised himself that he would control himself.

"Let's just enjoy the picnic food before I lose control of my senses," Katelyn whispered as she fought to catch her breath. This man truly was driving her to no return.

They sat down opposite each other on the blanket and while they enjoyed the food, Rolland proceeded to tell Katelyn about his week in Victoria. Katelyn shared with him about her study on the different native tribes, and how she had dreamed of Many Scars the Blackfoot Shaman going to each tribe in search of greater wisdom about the Great Spirit.

They left the park after there picnic lunch, because Rolland wanted to get unpacked, and Katelyn felt it would also be better that way. Her hormones were in an uproar and she need to settle herself down and get a hold of her emotions. After all, they would see each other in a few hours again.

Later in the evening, Rolland took Katelyn out for a nice dinner. They talked about Rolland's future and how his clientele was growing, and how the firm appreciated the efforts Rolland put into building the business up. Katelyn was happy that Rolland's dream was excelling, and longed for a letter from Victoria, so her dream could also be fulfilled. Oh how she admired this man.

CHAPTER FIFTEEN

THE NEXT MONTH WENT by rather quickly, and although her deep desire for Rolland increased with the passing of time, they tried hard not to be alone except when Rolland brought her home. A few times she had yearned to ask him to come into her apartment for a while, but she knew better than to do that. A long time ago, she had made herself a promise not to let any boy in her apartment by himself. Some of her friends had called her a coward, but these same friends looked at her today with envy. Her's was a life of challenge, because it was a challenge in today's society to refrain from sex. It wasn't easy, because she had the same desires as any normal person, but at least she had the guts to be abnormal according to today's standards.

Katelyn went to her mail box on June 27, and as she pulled out the one and only envelope that was there, she stared at the return address. The envelope had come from the museum in Victoria. Tearing it open, she pulled out the letter and quickly scanned it before reading the whole thing. What caught her eye was the words, 'You have been accepted to come and work at the Victoria Museum.' In all her excitement, she forgot where she was as she gave a shout of happiness. Once inside her apartment, she read the whole letter through completely.

She could hardly contain the excitement as she dialled Rollands number. The phone rang four times, before it went to his mail box, she hung up and dialled his cell phone number. When he answered the call, she was so excited that she could hardly speak.

"Hello, Rolland speaking."

Her breathing over the phone caused Rolland a bit of concern as he asked, "Sweetie, are you alright?"

"Yes Honey," I'm alright. "It's here!" Katelyn blurted out

"What's all the excitement about? What's here?" Rolland wanted to know.

"They want me to come and work in Victoria," Katelyn burst into tears.

"Sweetie," Rolland was taken back by Katelyn sobbing, "That's good news, but when do you start?"

"As soon as I can get there," Katelyn sniffled as she spoke.

"This calls for a celebration. How about we go out for steak and lobster tonight,." Rolland wasn't sure at that moment what else to say.

"I have to work tonight, but we could do it tomorrow night since it is Saturday, and I'm off this weekend."

"Alright Sweetie, it's a date for tomorrow night then." Rolland assured her.

"I'll be ready for you Honey." Katelyn whispered.

At work that evening, Katelyn could hardly keep her mind on her job. She gave her two week notice and her boss, though she hated to see Katelyn go, congratulated her and thanked her for the many years of dedicated work she had provided for the motel.

When Rolland pulled up to Katelyn's apartment the next evening, he was excited and yet nervous. It was as though he was taking Katelyn out for the first time. He wanted this dinner to be a lasting one for Katelyn. It was his desire that she be happy with life and everything that she did. This job in Victoria meant the world to Katelyn, and he was going to make sure that nothing would spoil that for her. Getting out of the car, he headed up the walk with his heart pounding for the love he had for Katelyn.

Suddenly the apartment door swung open, and there illuminated in the doorway stood the most beautiful princess in the whole world. Katelyn had taken the time to do up her hair. She had adorned herself with a blue dress, the kind one of the "Ladies" of old would have worn to a ballroom dance. Since she loved history, she sometimes collected relics from the past, and this dress was one of them. She didn't care if the dress was one from long ago, her life was her life, and she wasn't about to let the ways of society dictate to her what she should do or wear. Her life was one of the past, and if she wanted to act out that part in celebration, then it mattered not what others thought. Her second desire in life was to marry Rolland, and although it puzzled her why he hadn't asked her to marry him, maybe he would come to his senses after she was gone. She couldn't wait for him to make up his mind, 'What was he waiting for anyway.' Katelyn knew that her love for Rolland would never die, and after she was gone, Rolland might realize the mistake of letting her go to Victoria. She would have gladly stayed here if Rolland would marry her.

To Rolland, nothing in the world could have been more beautiful than Katelyn at that very moment. Not even one of the Seven Wonders of the World had anything to offer that could match her beauty. If there were eight wonders of the world, Katelyn's beauty would be number one. Maybe this would be a good time to ask her hand in marriage, but no, if he did that, then she might still change her mind about going to the job that her heart longed for. He knew that his heart would yearn for her after she was gone, but he also knew that he would have no problem obtaining a job for himself in Victoria, once the question was asked. His boss would put in a good recommendation for him when that time came. Right now, Katelyn must not know how he desired to ask her to marry him. It would be hard, but his love for her was so strong that he would force himself not to give her any inclination of his desire. His determination in college would help him through this time as well. He wanted her to be happy, and he believed that in time she would understand why he had waited as long as he did.

Stretching out his hand to her he spoke with pride, "Madam! A thousand sunsets could never match your beauty."

Blushing, Katelyn responded, "My Lord! How sweet are the words you speak to me this night."

Katelyn was in her glory. Not only did she get the job in Victoria, she was going out with the most eloquent man that she thought ever lived. Nothing was going to spoil the evening with her man as they celebrated this special occasion. She had looked forward to this day for a long time, and the only thing that could have changed her mind to leave would have been a proposal from Rolland. Her heart throbbed with desire to be with him the rest of her life, but he would always be in her heart just like Jack had been in Rose's heart all those years.

The evening passed by with much joy and laughter. If anyone thought Katelyn was out of place in her fancy dress, it made no difference to either of them. This was a day of celebration for Katelyn, and Rolland meant to make it worth her while. Maybe it was because Katelyn dwelt on the past so much, but the way she was dressed was the way Rolland thought all women should dress. They looked so much more ladylike and delicate in dresses.

After dinner was over, they went to Henderson Park for a stroll around the lake. Many heads turned to look at Katelyn as they walked slowly along the path. For Katelyn it was a time in bygone days where she was walking out in the meadow with Rolland. To her, there were only the two of them lost in each others love. She knew that they would have to be careful, and stay where there were people around at all times. As they walked together along the path around the lake, they met fewer and fewer people and Katelyn started to feel nervous. Her excitement about the job in Victoria might cloud her judgment if they didn't get back to where there were more people

The sun was beginning to set when they stood on the curved bridge that crossed over the water to the island just out of reach from the main body of land. The western sky was lined with an array of dazzling colours. Katelyn faced Rolland and looked longingly into his eyes. 'Why can you not ask me to marry you?' she was thinking.

"Honey," she smiled at him, "Thank you for the lovely dinner and evening."

"It is the least I could do for the lady that I love," Rolland smiled back at her.

The least is right, Katelyn thought. If you asked me to marry you, that would be the ultimate. She respected Rolland for the stand he had taken as far as going all the way with her. That had been her request when they first started dating, and he had agreed that it was the proper way to go. Even though they had almost lost it a couple times, they had been able to get control before it was to late, but why, if his love for her was so great, didn't he propose to her. He wasn't at all like other guys who had dropped her for not having sex with them, so there must be some feelings there for her. The question that kept on haunting her was, 'Why?'

"I love you Honey," Katelyn whispered as she gave him a peck on the lips.

Rolland reached his arms around her and pulled her body towards himself. He could feel her breasts heave as he held her tightly against his own body. He was filled with ravishing love for this young lady, and it was his desire that they could be together forever, but he wanted their relationship to be more than just for sex. His love and respect went deeper than his desire for her body, although at that moment his mind was lost and out of control with desire to end this evening in rapturous bliss. His desire to ask her hand in marriage almost slipped out, but it would be wrong for him to become selfish and want Katelyn to stay with him instead of pursuing her career.

"Sweetie, there will never be any other that could fill your place in my life," Rolland assured her and then proceeded to kiss her passionately.

Katelyn's breasts became firm and her nipples hardened, as her body yearned to make love to Rolland. Gone was the reality of where they were. Pulling Rolland off the bridge, they lay down on the soft grass of the island, and Katelyn began tearing at Rollands shirt as his hand gently began moving up the front of her dress. As his hands reached her breasts, Kately sighed with anticipation. Yes, she was finally going to experience the ultimate with Rolland.

The picture of Rose and Jack in the back of the car flashed through Katelyn's mind again. Wrenching herself free from Rollands grip her breath coming out in short sharp gasps she managed to say, "No! Rolland, we can't."

Rollands chest heaved as he tried to control his breathing. How Katelyn knew the right time to stop was a mystery to him. He was in a moment of no turning back, when she stopped them. Being ever so thankful for her quick thinking, Rolland sighed with relief. He had even forgotten where he was. What an embarrassment that could have been.

"Thank you Sweetie," he spoke softly as he looked at her.

As they walked back to the car, neither one said a word. The excitement on the bridge had left them both longing for the other. It wasn't until they reached the car and Rolland opened the door for Katelyn that she spoke.

"Honey, you are the most caring man in the whole world."

"Thank you Sweetie," Rolland replied, "But why would you say that?"

"You treat me with respect," Katelyn kissed him before getting into the car.

As Rolland walked around the car to the drivers side, he couldn't help but admire Katelyn for who she was and for the strong will she had. If she hadn't pulled away from him, he would not have been able to stop himself. Still wondering about how she did it, Rolland got into the car and looking at her he asked.

"Sweetie! How did you manage to stop us from going to far? Didn't you desire to have me at that moment?"

"Rolland Honey," Katelyn reached over and took his hand in hers. "Tonight I didn't care how far we went. The thing that stopped me was our commitment to each other."

"But how could you remember the commitment when we were locked in the arms of love and passion at the point of no return."

"I had a flash back of Rose and Jack in the back seat of the car," Katelyn breathed heavily.

"That put a stop to us going all the way!" Rolland sight with relief.

"Yes Honey," Katelyn squeezed his hand, "That was the second time I had that flash back."

"Am I ever thankful that you are a dreamer, because I could never have stopped us tonight." Rolland smiled at her as he started the car.

"But Honey, you also stopped us one night while we were in Indian Battle Park," Katelyn insisted.

"Yes Sweetie," Rolland laughed, "That night I remembered, just in time, the commitment I made to you. I could not dishonour you by rejecting that commitment, but tonight my mind was in a fog as I couldn't help admiring your beauty."

"Rolland Honey," Katelyn smiled at him, "I will love you till the end of time."

Back in her apartment, Katelyn stood again looking out of her window. "Rose," she spoke to the reflection of herself in the window pane, "I guess you were braver than I am. I could have experienced what you did, but now I might never know what you felt that night as you were passionately embraced together in eternal ecstasy."

"Rolland," she spoke sadly to her reflection in the window. "You could have stopped me from going to Victoria."

That night as she slept, Katelyn again dreamed of Rolland carrying her away, but never proposing to her. This time she didn't wake up in a cold sweat, but rather she slept peacefully. If Rolland didn't propose to her, she would still love him the same. She would just have to be like Pretty Bird, Running Wild was not the most important in her life anymore after her quest. Rolland would just have to be placed on the back burner, for the time being at least. Her dream was being fulfilled as she was headed for Victoria.

When she woke in the morning, she thought about the dreams, and again she spoke out loud, "Well Rose, my man didn't propose to me, so I will just hide my love for him in my heart like you did with Jack, except without the intimate bliss you experienced."

For the next two weeks Katelyn was busy getting things ready for the move. Rolland helped her the best he could without being in the way. He decided to go to the airport and get Katelyn's ticket arranged for the trip. Then the day of departure finally arrived.

For Katelyn this was the day she had longed for, and yet dreaded. She would be moving ahead in life, but at the same time there would be all those friends and good times that she was leaving behind. The one thing she had wished for didn't happen, but she knew that she could never forget Rolland. He would always hold a special place in her heart, and she would see him from time to time on his trips to Victoria.

When they arrived at the airport, Rolland got her bags and took them over to the check out counter. After the bags were tagged and put on the conveyer belt to be placed on the proper flight, there was still plenty of time to have some coffee before departure. They talked about Katelyn's new job, and how they would write emails to each other every day.

When the time for departure came, Katelyn threw her arms around Rollands neck. Her eyes were moist and tears began to trickle down her cheeks. She did not bother to wipe them away, because she didn't mind that Rolland could see how she felt about him. Even as she hugged him and held his body close to hers, she couldn't help thinking, 'If only Rolland would propose to her, she could still change her mind about boarding the plane.'

"Honey," Katelyn whispered in his ear, I'll never want another man the way I want you."

"I love you more than you could ever imagine," Rolland replied as he gently brushed his lips against hers.

Katelyn wanted to say to him, 'You love me, but you don't want to marry me,' but she knew that was not the right thing to say. Rolland had his own reason for not asking her hand in marriage, and Katelyn respected his personal feelings. After all, marriage was a big commitment and maybe Rolland wasn't ready for such a commitment yet. Maybe it scared him. With one final kiss, she headed down the corridor to catch her flight.

She had requested a window seat, and as she sat down her eyes looked longingly toward the building in hopes of getting one last glimpse of Rolland standing by a window. They were too far away to make out the faces of those peering out at them.

Suddenly the stewardess was leaning over and saying, "Miss. Melroy."

Katelyn looked at the stewardess and answered, "Yes. I am Katelyn Melroy."

"Well Miss. Melroy," the stewardess proceeded, "There is a call for you on the ship to shore telephone. Would you please follow me."

Katelyn got up and followed the stewardess to where the phone was. She was puzzled at why someone would call her at this time. Picking up the receiver, she said, "Hello, Katelyn here."

"Katelyn Melroy will you marry me?" Rollands voice came through the receiver.

"Rolland!" Katelyn was flabbergasted to hear his voice, because she had just left his side. "Why now? Why couldn't you have asked before I boarded the plane?"

"Sweetie, I would have asked you before," Rollands voice came back, "but I was concerned that you would forfeit your job in Victoria if I did that."

"Honey you are so thoughtful, and so caring," Katelyn breathed softly into the phone.

"You didn't answer my question Sweetie. Will you marry me?" Rolland asked again.

Katelyn burst into tears of joy as she spoke, "Yes Honey, I'll marry you. In fact, I'll leave the plane right now to be with you."

"Sweetie," Rolland was overjoyed, "You don't have to leave the plane. Please tell the stewardess, who called you to the phone, that you will marry me."

Katelyn didn't understand why Rolland would ask her to do such a thing, but in her excitement she would have done anything for him at this time. Beckoning the stewardess to come over, Katelyn said, "I'm going to marry Rolland!"

The stewardess smiled and pulling open a cupboard door, she withdrew a bouquet of twelve long stemed roses and handed them to Katelyn. Tied to one of the rose stems was a diamond engagement ring. Katelyn's eyes nearly popped out of their sockets as she saw the ring. She was so overcome with joy that it was hard for her to speak, but she managed to say before bursting into an array of tears, "Rolland Honey, I love you so much, but how did you pull this off, and why can't I come off the plane to be with you."

"It was easy Sweetie. Rolland laughed. "I did it the day I booked your flight. It cost me a bit of money to hold the plane for a few minutes longer, but for you Sweetie, it was more than worth it."

"But I'm on my way to Victoria now," Katelyn sobbed. "When did you plan to get married?"

"When I move to Victoria," Rolland laughed.

"What do you mean, when you move to Victoria," Katelyn blubbered in her excitement.

"It was hard to keep this as a surprise," Rolland replied. "I'm moving to Victoria to run the new office the firm opened up there last week. They offered the job to me because I told them I was quitting to find a new job in Victoria so I could be with you."

"Oh my Darling Rolland. How could I have ever doubted you." Katelyn cried.

"See you soon in Victoria Sweetie," Rolland sang out with joy.

"Rolland you are such a wonderful man, I can hardly wait to have you by my side for all times," she burst into a new array of tears. "See you soon."

As Katelyn returned to the seat, her smile radiated her face. 'What a considerate rascal Rolland had been' she thought, 'To wait until this moment to spring the question to her.' Her heart pounded with excitement as she sat down.

The Captains voice came over the P.A., "Ladies and gentlemen, we are ready for take off. The slight delay we experienced was due to the fact that a young lady by the name of Katelyn Melroy received a proposal of marriage over the phone, and she accepted just moments ago. Congratulations Katelyn from the Captain and the crew." The plane was filled with cheers as the people rejoiced with Katelyn.

Katelyn settled back in her seat as the plane taxied down the runway. She was going to be the happiest person on the face of the earth, because of her Rolland. He had thought about her career and her future before his desire to marry her. He always considered her feelings first, and she admired him for that. Now she could also put closure on the life of Pretty Bird and Running Wild, even though she wasn't laying under the Cottonwood tree to dream about it.

"Well Rose," she said as she closed her eyes, "You have nothing over me now. Soon I will experience what you felt like in Jacks arms that night."

The lady in the seat next to Katelyn looked at her in astonishment, "Pardon me!" she said.

Katelyn didn't even open her eyes, but she laughed as she said, "It's okay Madam, you had to have been there."

THE END

Printed in the United States
By Bookmasters